Hemmed In

Hemmed In

A Quilters Club Mystery

Marjory Sorrell Rockwell

ABSOLUTELY AMA⚡ING eBOOKS

ABSOLUTELY AMAZING eBOOKS

For information contact:
Publisher@AbsolutelyAmazingEbooks.com
ISBN-13: 978-1493610068
ISBN-10: 1493610066

"Our lives are like quilts – bits and pieces, joy and sorrow, stitched with love."

- Anonymous

Hemmed In

Chapter One

The Mad Matilda Wilkins Quilt

Turns out that Maddy Madison missed Tuesday's gathering of the Quilters Club because she had to drive to Indianapolis to pick up her grandson, N'yen. Bill and Kathy had adopted the boy last year. Just turning nine, he'd asked to visit "Grammy and Grampy" as his birthday present. Which meant that he really wanted to see his favorite cousin, eleven-year-old Agnes.

Aggie was an honorary member of the Quilters Club and N'yen wanted to join too. The kids saw it as an undercover detective agency, being that its members – Maddy Madison, Lizzie Ridenour, Bootsie Purdue, and Cookie Bentley – had solved a couple of local crimes last year.

However, the four members of the Quilters Club saw it as ... well, a quilter's club. The crime solving had been incidental.

Aggie and her mom had joined Maddy for the drive to Indianapolis (a two-hour journey each way) to pick up the boy. As a result, they missed the biggest robbery that had ever taken place in Caruthers Corners – the theft of the Mad Matilda Wilkins quilt, a patchwork masterpiece that had hung in the lobby of the Town Hall for over one hundred years.

The quilt had been appraised at $100,000 ... but to the good folks of Caruthers Corners it was priceless.

Back in 1897, Matilda Wilkins had hand-stitched this wondrous patchwork creation, a scene that might have been conceived by Hieronymus Bosch. There on the fabric danced angels and demons, sinners and saints. The border was decorated with odd symbols that some thought might be a secret code, supposedly the language of Satan himself. You see, Mad Matilda was known to be a witch.

She had lived on Cloven Hoof Lane, so-named in deference to its only resident. Her cottage had been located at the end of the narrow dirt road. Once a stone structure with a slumping roof, the cottage has long since fallen to the ground.

Nonetheless, visitors like to drive out to look at the scattered stones and the well where she is said to have died, refusing to float, as witches are wont to do.

The religious zealots who tossed Mad Matilda into the 80-foot well were never officially identified, but legend had it they were members of a snake-handling cult that maintained a house of worship over near the Never Ending Swamp. Other than the leader – Rev. Billingsley Royce – the identities of its members are a forgotten part of history. There's no sign of the church today, its exact location debated by old-timers.

Mad Matilda's patchwork quilt had been rescued from the crumbling cottage by a distant relative and donated to the Caruthers Corners Historical Society. Thereafter, the quilt has been displayed in the lobby of the Town Hall as a decorative wall hanging – its satanic history ignored, its craftsmanship admired.

Quilting Bee magazine once called it "the best example of allegorical quilt design extent in Indiana." Many museums had offered to buy it, but the Historical Society refused to sell this piece of the town's heritage.

For over five generations the 8' x 8' *objet d'art*

had loomed over visitors to the Town Hall, accepted as an oddity, but nonetheless mesmerizing in its intricate design.

Then it was stolen.

There one day, gone the next – the very date that N'yen Madison had turned nine. Of course, there was no connection. Or was there?

Chapter Two

The Quilters Club On the Case

Caruthers Corners had been founded in 1829 by three stranded fur trappers. One of them, a sour and dyspeptic man named Jacob Caruthers, had lent his name to the town that grew up on this very spot. The other had been a sneaky backstabber named Ferdinand Jinks. And the third had been a crusty old Indian fighter named Beauregard Madison. As it turns out, Col. Madison was the great-great grandfather of Beauregard Hollingsworth Madison IV, Maddy's husband – and the town's current mayor.

"This will be the ruination of me," groaned Beau as he sat at the kitchen table, head cradled in his arms. His wife had just returned from the airport in Indianapolis with young N'yen in tow. She was shocked by the news. The Wilkins Witch Quilt was one of the town's claims to fame, that and its annual watermelon festival.

With a population of only 2,577 (not counting N'yen's singular visit), the town got more recognition than you'd expect. Watermelon Days had been featured last year on *The Today Show*, with Al Roker entering the watermelon-eating contest. He came in 63 out of 87 contestants.

Beau had just finished reciting the known facts: The quilt had been in its place on the wall in the lobby when he locked the Town Hall last night. It was gone when he opened up this morning. The alarm had not been tripped.

Police Chief Jim Purdue was baffled. He was more used to handing out parking tickets along the town's two-block business district than solving art thefts. Jim was Beau Madison's best friend and the husband of Maddy's pal Bootsie. "I've called in the state boys," he said, patting Beau reassuringly on the shoulder.

The kitchen was crowded – Beau, Jim, Maddy, Bootsie, daughter Tilly and her husband Mark. Even Cookie and Lizzie. Plus the kids, Aggie and N'yen. The Vietnamese boy's parent's had entrusted him to the airlines for the trip, allowing the Chicago couple to enjoy a mid-week vacation at the Wisconsin Dells.

Tilly's hubby was also the town's attorney.

Mark the Shark (as he was known to the family) had been a big-time Los Angeles lawyer before downsizing his life and moving back to the ol' hometown. "I spoke to the SBI this afternoon," he reported. "They're sending in an electronics expert first thing in the morning. Said they want to figure out how the perp bypassed the alarm system."

"Perp?" asked Tilly.

"Perpetrator," Jim Purdue explained the verbal shorthand.

"The SBI says –" Mark Tidemore continued.

"SBI?" interrupted Tilly.

"The State Bureau of Investigation," Jim translated.

Mark plowed on, "– says the alarm was still set, no signs of forced entry, no clues whatsoever. They can't figure out how the quilt was stolen."

"That makes two of us," sighed the police chief.

"Beats me too," nodded Beau. "That quilt disappeared as if by magic."

"Of course, it was magic," giggled little Aggie. "The woman who made it was a witch."

"Aggie!" scolded her mother.

"That's what my Sunday School teacher said."

"There is no such thing as a witch," her mother corrected.

"Didn't you say the lady who runs the Clothes Horse Boutique is a witch?" That was a small dress shop on Main Street owned by Missy Yager. Missy was a former Watermelon Days Queen (1998).

"That's because she said I was fat."

"Missy said that?" exclaimed Tilly's mother.

"Not exactly. She suggested I needed to go up a dress size."

"That was after the second baby," her husband pointed out. "You've lost all that extra weight."

"What? You think I'm fat too?"

Mark rolled his eyes, sensing a no-win conversation. "You look perfect, hon."

Maddy turned to her granddaughter. "Sometimes people call each other names when they get upset. But that doesn't mean Missy Yager is *actually* a witch on a broomstick."

"Like the ones at Halloween?" asked Aggie.

"That's just pretend," said Maddy. "Like ghosts and goblins."

"If there aren't real ghosts, how does a dead person float up to Heaven?"

"We'll talk about that later," grinned Maddy.

"But as far as the quilt's disappearance is concerned, it has nothing to do with magic."

"That's right, honey," said Jim Purdue. "When I said 'magic' I was just exaggerating."

Aggie wrinkled her forehead. "Exaggerating?"

"Stretching the truth," explained Maddy.

"Well, yeah," grunted Jim.

Mark the Shark stated the obvious: "We still have to figure out how the thief managed to steal that quilt."

"Don't worry," said N'yen. "The Quilters Club will solve this case."

Chapter Three

An Inside Job

Police Chief Jim Purdue shook his head. "Sorry, young man, but your grandmother and her friends are sitting this one out."

"Why?" pouted N'yen. "The Quilters Club could help you find the burglar."

"It's bad enough when the Quilters Club meddles in one of my cases, but the state boys won't hesitate to arrest them for interfering with a police investigation."

Aggie Tidemore frowned. "But aren't you the police, Uncle Jim?"

"Well, yes. But these are state police. Higher up the ladder than me. They're taking over the investigation."

"Why can't you just deputize the Quilters Club?" argued N'yen. "Let them handle it."

Maddy was trying hard to conceal her smile. "It doesn't work that way, dear. We are *ex officio*. Not official detectives."

"That's right," nodded the girl's grandfather. "You gals are just pretend detectives."

"Gals?" challenged N'yen. "What about me? I wanna be a pretend detective too."

Chief Purdue laughed. "Oh? What could you tell us about this case?"

The boy raised his chin defiantly. "Well, if nobody broke *into* Town Hall, maybe they broke *out* instead."

That stopped everyone.

"Hm, if someone knew the code, he could reset the alarm system from inside the building, giving him time to get out without setting off the bells and whistles," admitted Beau Madison.

"But what about the locked door?" said Mark the Shark.

"The deadbolt has a knob inside. You could unlock it, step outside and let it snap back into place," replied Beau.

"But you'd have to be inside the building to begin with," argued the police chief.

Beau thought for a moment. "I suppose someone could have hidden in a restroom," he said. "Can't say that I checked them before leaving last night."

"An inside job," exclaimed Bootsie.

"Now don't go saying that," Jim Purdue warned his wife. "Anybody could have gone into the building during office hours and hidden out in the restroom."

"That's what I meant. Someone *inside* the building."

Beau thought about it. "If it really was an inside job, someone who works there, the list of suspects would be short – me, my secretary, the Town Clerk, and the Tax Assessor. The head of Building and Zoning was out sick, and the Director of Public Works is on vacation."

"What about the Town Planner?" asked Bootsie.

Beau shrugged. "We don't have one at the moment, not since Joe Johansson went to meet his maker last month."

"Oh, that's right," she nodded. "He's the fellow who stuck his finger in the light socket while changing a bulb. I don't think I ever met him."

"Joe was new to town," answered Beau. "I'd just hired him down from Gary. He was moving into his house on Rocking Chair Lane when it happened. Blew out the circuits on that side of town. They were without electricity for two whole days."

"I remember," said Maddy. "The funeral home is on that side of town so the refrigeration was out. They had to store his body at the ice plant till the electricity came back on."

"First, we need to establish alibis for all the town employees," said Mark. Liability insurance would kick in, if one of the officials were at fault.

"Me, I was here last night," said Beau.

Maddy nodded. "I can vouch for that. This isn't like the time Beau stole that statue of his great-great grandfather."

"That was different," muttered Beau. "It was a ploy to immortalize my forbearer."

Jim Purdue waved away their words. "You're not under suspicion, Beau. You're the mayor, for goodness sake."

"The last mayor was a crook," Beau pointed out. Not looking for any favoritism.

"But you're not," the police chief ended the discussion. "Besides, you have a reliable witness vouching for your whereabouts – your wife."

"That's right," said Maddy. "I barely slept last night, anticipating N'yen's arrival. I can attest you were in bed beside me – except for two trips to the bathroom. That nervous bladder of yours."

"We'd better clear the other town officials," Beau quickly changed the subject from his bladder, "so the state boys can focus on real suspects."

"And we need to make a list of everyone they can recall being in the building yesterday," added Jim Purdue. "I'd better interview them while memories are fresh."

"I can't believe the Wilkins Witch Quilt has been stolen," said Bootsie.

"Yes, it's an irreplaceable heirloom," nodded Cookie.

"Valuable too," added Lizzie.

"True," agreed Maddy. "A hundred thousand dollars is nothing to sneeze at."

"Point well taken," sighed Beau Madison. "Guess we'd better put surveillance cameras back into next year's budget."

Chapter Four

Rev. Royce and the
Church of Avenging Angels

In addition to being a member of the Quilters Club, Cookie Bentley served as head of the Caruthers Corners Historical Society. So it was no surprise to her friends that she knew all the sordid details about Mad Matilda Wilkins – the town's alleged witch.

The Quilters Club had gathered in the cramped quarters of the Historical Society to conspire. Despite last night's warning, they couldn't resist looking into the theft.

"Yes, Matilda Wilkins was certifiably mad," Cookie affirmed, sitting there behind her antique desk. "The old woman truly believed she was a witch. People came to her to buy love potions, have her to cast spells on their enemies, and predict their future. By all accounts these occult activities made her quite wealthy. But no money was found after her death. Everybody assumed that those fanatics who murdered her took it."

"Why didn't they take the quilt?" asked Liz Ridenour. Being a banker's wife, she always thought in monetary terms.

"We value it today, but back then it was just a fancy bedspread," explained Cookie. "Besides, all those symbols on the quilt may have scared them. It was said Mad Matilda used it in satanic ccremonies."

"Why didn't those people who murdered her get arrested?" asked Bootsie. As the wife of the police chief, she was curious about such details.

Cookie patted a stack of yellowed newspapers. "According to contemporary reports, all the members of the Church of Avenging Angels left the county in the dark of night. None were ever captured."

"Church of Avenging Angels?" repeated Maddy. "That sounds quite ominous."

"They were an extremist cult. Believed that violence against evil was justified. Hunted down witches." She pulled a faded photograph out a drawer. "This is Rev. Billingsley Royce, leader of the Avenging Angels. If anybody got Matilda

Wilkins's money, it was this guy."

Maddy leaned forward to study the photo. The man had close-set eyes and spikey, unkempt hair. His pointed chin looked very defiant. A wine-stain birthmark covered half his forehead. He held a coiled snake in his hands. "Scary looking," she observed.

"Rev. Royce may have been crazier than Mad Matilda. It's said he slept in a bed of rattlesnakes. But I suspect that's just a tall tale," added Cookie.

"What does any of this have to do with the stolen quilt?" scowled Lizzie Ridenour. The redhead had a short attention span.

"Maybe nothing," admitted Cookie, pushing her wire-rimmed granny glasses back upon the bridge of her thin nose. "But knowing the quilt's history may be helpful in recovering it."

"We're going to recover it?"

"Don't you think we should?" responded Cookie.

"Of course," said Maddy. "After all, we know more about quilts than the State Bureau of Investigation."

"Jim's not going to like this," muttered the police chief's wife.

Maddy patted her friend's shoulder. "Then

don't tell him. No need to worry your husband unnecessarily. That's my policy."

"One rumor had it that Matilda Wilkins's money was buried under the church's doorstep, awaiting Rev. Royce's return."

"Surely people have looked there," said Bootsie.

"Not really," Cookie shook her head. Her mousey brown hair glinted with gold from the overhead light. "You see, when the Avenging Angels pulled out, they burned their church to the ground. Or so it was claimed. It could be that the deputized posse looking for them burnt it. After all these years, nobody seems to remember exactly where it was located."

"How could you lose a church?"

"The town plats are pretty accurate, but no one paid much attention to the surrounding countryside back then. Old newspaper articles say it was on the far side of the Never Ending Swamp, but that's a lot of empty land. Mostly watermelon fields today."

"Okay, then let's concentrate on the quilt," decided Maddy. "Do you know if Mad Matilda made others?"

Cookie shook head. "Not as far as we know.

'The Battle Between Heaven and Hell' was the only one."

"Wow! That's a pretty dramatic name," exclaimed Bootsie.

"That's the official title given to the Wilkins quilt."

"I didn't know that," Lizzie admitted. "I've always heard it referred to as the Wilkins Witch Quilt."

"The official title is posted there on a little bronze plaque in the Town Hall," admonished Cookie. "Anyone could read it if they had a mind to do so."

"I hardly ever go to the Town Hall," rejoined the redhead, sounding a little defensive.

"The title comes from the design on the quilt, angels and demons fighting it out. An apocalyptic vision." Cookie pulled out a color photograph of the quilt, taken when it was still hanging on the Town Hall wall. "It's quite detailed."

The four women studied the picture. The orange-and-red quilt was dazzling to the eye. Each patchwork square was embroidered with tiny figures, some bearing wings, others displaying horns, with monsters scattered among them – like a scene from a Civil War battle, but being fought with otherworldly soldiers.

"Ooo-ee," said Lizzie. "I've never looked at the quilt up-close before. Reminds me of a nightmare I might have after eating too much pistachio ice cream."

"There's no such thing as too much pistachio ice cream," muttered Bootsie, a frequent visitor to the DQ on Main Street. She suffered a little weight problem from time to time.

Cookie described the scene: "Angels attacking devils with thunderbolts. Devils wielding pitchforks. Goblins and half-human monsters gnawing on angels' legs. Cauldrons boiling with witches' brew, fires burning, thunderclouds spewing lightning, the very earth splitting to swallow combatants, all hell breaking loose!"

"What an imagination," observed Maddy.

"Matilda Wilkins claimed it was a vision of things to come."

"Well, it's now more than a hundred years later and I haven't noticed any strangers with wings or horns hanging around the gazebo in the town square," smirked Lizzie. She and her husband Edgar owned that big Victorian house facing the grassy expanse of the square.

"Don't scoff," admonished Bootsie. It wasn't clear whether she was being superstitious or just overly reverent.

"What about these strange markings around the border?" Maddy pointed. "Do you know what they mean?"

Cookie pulled out a thick book titled *A History of Caruthers Corners and Surrounding Environs* by Martin J. Caruthers. He'd been the father of the former mayor, the scallywag that Beau had defeated in a landslide victory. "Let me read this. Old Martin Caruthers devoted a few paragraphs to the Wilkins quilt."

Fitting her reading glasses over the narrow bridge of her nose, Cookie continued:

"Whereupon an elderly crone named Matilda Elizabeth Wilkins lived on the outskirts of town, we come to a discussion of her subsequent murder and the patchwork prize she left behind. Said to be a sorcerer, Mrs. Wilkins sold magic potions to the lovelorn and vengefuyl. Thus, a religious sect known as the Avenging Angels is thought to have kill't her. The followers scattered and were never tried for the heinous crime, drowning the old woman in her own water well.

"A relative rescued a wondrous quilt, purported to be a magical device, from her cottage and turned it over to one of the town fathers (that being my biological pater familias), who preserved it for all to see on display in the governmental building facing the square.

"This quilt was said to bestow the aspect of invisibility upon its owner. It is embroidered with scenes of the Armageddon, depicting the final battle between Good and Evil. Around the border are indecipherable symbols, thought to be a secret language known only to practitioners of the Dark Arts. Despite its frightening subject matter, the Matilda Wilkins Quilt is an example of superb needlework. It is deserving of preservation as an ignoble chapter in this town's history, as well as a record of the masterful craftsmanship of its inhabitants."

"Indecipherable,' the old man said." Bootsie looked frustrated. She liked things to be black and white.

"Those markings *must* have some meaning," insisted Lizzie. "Has anyone ever called in a language or code expert?"

Cookie pulled out a clipping. "Says here that back in the '40s a World War II code breaker took a look at the quit but was stymied."

"These markings look like they could be ancient runes or cuneiform writing," said Maddy. "Maybe it's not a code at all. Just some kind of little-known hieroglyphics."

Bootsie said, "Why not ask Daniel Sokolowski? He has lots of sources when it comes to things like this." Sokolowski was owner of Dan's Den of Antiquity, a crowded little shop on Main Street that displayed Tiffany lamps, Chippendale chairs, carousel horses, and a genuine Tlingit totem pole that came all the way from Alaska.

"Surely someone would have recognized it by now," argued Cookie, not eager to gallop off on a wild goose chase. But when Maddy nodded her head at the suggestion, she knew the plan was approved. The mayor's wife was sort of the unofficial leader of the Quilters Club.

Chapter Five

An Accident in Wisconsin

The Quilters Club's plan to consult Daniel Sokolowski went astray when Maddy got the phone call from Wisconsin. Bill and Kathy had been in an automobile accident on the way back from the Dells. Her son had a broken leg, his wife a fractured hip. They were in the Aurora St. Luke's Medical Center, ranked #2 out of 153 hospitals in that state.

"No, don't fly up here, mom," Bill said firmly. "Kathy and I are getting good care. We just want to make sure you're okay with N'yen staying with you and dad for a few weeks. Give me and Kathy time to get back on our feet. So to speak." Her son had a way of laughing at adversity.

"Of course," Maddy replied. "You know how fond we are of N'yen. And he loves being here with Aggie. They're inseparable."

"Thanks, mom."

"Nonetheless, I think I should fly up there for a day, just to check on your medical care and help with anything you might need. N'yen can spend the night at Aggie's. Your sister Tilly won't mind."

"One day. No more. You know how fidgety dad gets when you leave him to fend for himself."

"I'll head to the airport in Indy this afternoon. You're sure you two are all right?"

"As they say, sticks and stone can break my bones. Apparently an eighteen-wheeler can do that too. My femur got cracked, my nose got bloodied, Kathy broke her hip, and the Subaru was totaled. Thank goodness for airbags – and Subaru's reinforced frame body structure!"

≈ ≈ ≈

Maddy was actually gone for three days. By the time she returned from Milwaukee, the Indiana State Bureau of Investigation had determined that the thief had hidden inside the Town Hall until after hours, removed the quilt from the wall using a step ladder stored in the janitor's closet, reset the alarm, then slipped out into the night.

A brilliant deduction.

Just as N'yen had said.

The SBI questioned the boy to determine how

he knew the *modus operandi* of the thief, but gave up after he described the plot of a movie called *Flawless* in which a janitor robs a diamond distributor, an inside job.

They did, however, give Jasper Beanie a hard time. In addition to being the cemetery's caretaker, Jasper acted as the Town Hall's janitor. Fortunately for him, he only worked on Wednesdays and Fridays, so he wasn't there that Monday when a culprit had hidden inside the building to rob it.

Chief Purdue cleared all the town officials.

Like Beau Madison, the Town Clerk had been home with his wife ... and new baby. Being colicky, the tot had kept the couple up half the night.

The Tax Assessor had played poker with his cronies until 3 in the morning, then sacked out on his friend's couch. Divorced, he didn't have to report home to a wife.

Becky Marsch, Beau's new secretary, had spent the night with her boyfriend, though she'd been reluctant to admit the affair. After all, this was a small town.

Jim Purdue had also phoned Big Elk Lodge, the resort in Idaho where the director of Public

Works was vacationing. Turns out, George Wilkerson had bagged an elk on Tuesday. Got his picture in the *Big Elk Gazette*.

And Doc Habegger confirmed that Ferdinand Gilmore, the Planning and Zoning guy, was in bed with a temperature of 102°. "If he's able to go out and steal quilts, it'd be a modern-day medical miracle," the doctor had said.

The list of people who had been in the Town Hall on Monday was lengthy. Even so, many visitors were likely overlooked. With property taxes coming due, Arthur Rutledge had processed 127 payments that day despite his usual hangover.

Rutledge printed out the list of people he'd processed, but he couldn't be sure who had accompanied them – wives, brothers, miscellaneous friends.

The Town Clerk added 32 names to the list. And Becky contributed 13 more from Beau's appointment book.

The SBI was studying all the names with the diligence of high school seniors cramming for their final exam.

"The state boy's will never catch the crook this way," Beau told his wife over supper. What with N'yen and Aggie joining them, watermelon à la mode was on the desert menu.

"Why not?" Maddy asked.

"Too many suspects. If the Wilkins Witch Quilt is ever recovered, it will likely be by some unscrupulous art fence turning in the seller for a fat reward."

≈ ≈ ≈

After dinner (the chili was great!), the phone rang. Aggie was first to pick it up. "Madison residence," she said with the aplomb of an experienced receptionist. "Whom may I say is calling?"

It was one of the state boys, a gruff agent known behind his back as The Nail. Lieutenant Neil Wannamaker was acting as lead investigator on the case. Aggie handed the phone to her grandfather, whispering, "It's a man named Wanna-something. He sounds scary."

Beau took the phone. "Yes, Lt. Wannamaker, I'd be happy to go over my appointments with you. But all the names on that list are leading citizens. I'd vouch for each and every one of the people I met with on Monday. First thing in the morning at my office? Fine."

"A waste of time," Beau grunted as he put the phone down. "But gotta go through the motions, I suppose."

"*Some*body stole that quilt," Maddy reminded him. "I just hope it's not anyone we know."

Chapter Six

At the Ruins of the Wilkins Cottage

The next morning the Quilters Club – the four women and little Aggie – set out on a field trip to inspect the ruins of the Wilkins cottage. N'yen was at home pouting, seeing his exclusion as nothing short of sexism, girls ganging up against the lone boy.

About a half-hour north of Caruthers Corners, Maddy turned her big SUV onto a sandy road that cut through flat watermelon fields belonging to Aitkens Produce, the biggest farm in the county. About four miles in they came to an oasis in the farmland, a cluster of oak trees that shaded a stonewalled well. Someone – Boyd Aitkens most likely – had installed a pump to draw water up to a large cattle trough. Not that there were any cows in sight.

"Over there," Cookie pointed. "That clump of

rocks must be where the house stood."

They strolled over to inspect the remains of Matilda Wilkins's cottage. Most of the foundation stones had been carried away, probably to build some other structure on the watermelon farm.

Lizzie paced it off. "Not a very big house," she assayed its diminutive size.

Bootsie was peering into the well. "I can't see the bottom," she said.

"Don't lean too far," advised Maddy. "That didn't work out too well for Mad Matilda."

"Did people really kill her?" asked Aggie, still learning about the inhumanity of fellow humans.

"Bad people," Lizzie told her, red hair blowing in the breeze that came off the surrounding fields.

"Church people?" The girl had heard them talking.

"A cult," corrected Cookie. "The Avenging Angels were more like a gang of murders and thieves hiding under the cloak of piety."

"And nobody knows where their hideout was?" asked Aggie.

"Well, they called it a house of worship, but that was certainly a misnomer."

"Miss who?"

"Misnamed."

"Oh," said Aggie. Her blonde locks brushed her shoulders, a tomboy look. "Why don't we go find it? Didn't you say they buried the treasure there?"

Cookie cracked a smile. "One newspaper article speculated they buried the money they stole from Mad Matilda at the church. But there's no basis for it, other than a local farmer who claimed Rev. Royce told him that."

"Why would Rev. Royce tell anyone where he hid the money?" scoffed Maddy. "What would keep that farmer from digging it up for himself?"

"Good point," nodded the bank president's wife.

"What's this?" said Bootsie, still staring into the well. "Looks like some markings on the inside."

The women gathered round the well. "Markings?" said Cookie, straining to see. Her eyes followed Bootsie's pointed finger. There on some of the stones about three feet down were scratches that might have been writing of some kind.

"Hard to make out," muttered Lizzie. Afraid to lean over the rim. "It's awfully dark down there."

"I've got a flashlight in the glove

compartment," volunteered Maddy. "Hang on."

"Let me see the markings," begged Aggie, but her protective companions refused to let her near the open well.

"Better stand back," warned Lizzie. "It's dangerous." She stepped backward, away from the well, as if following her own advice."

"Awwww."

Maddy returned with a small penlight. It was more powerful than it looked. She aimed the beam at the scratches, tracing the indentions with the light. "Hm, could be the same kind of symbols that were on the quilt's border," she noted.

"Ruins?" said Aggie.

"I think you mean 'runes,' dear," Bootsie corrected.

"That reminds me," said Cookie. "We have an appointment this afternoon with Daniel Sokolowski. He's going to recommend someone who knows Old Norse writing."

"Why Norse?" asked Lizzie. "Didn't you say those markings could be Sumerian cuneiform writing or Egyptian hieroglyphics?"

Cookie glanced at the scratches before answering. "No, they're certainly not Egyptian hieroglyphics or Japanese kanji. Those forms of writing are more pictorial. As for cuneiforms, ancient Sumer was located a long way from Caruthers Corners. However, there is some evidence of Norsemen coming this way."

"Norsemen? You mean Vikings?"

Cookie nodded. Despite her plain-Jane hairstyle and spectacles, you could see she was a beauty underneath. "The Old Norse feminine noun *víking* refers to an expedition overseas. We know they came to Vinland – probably eastern Canada – around 1000 AD. And the Kensington Runestone was found in Douglas County, Minnesota, only seven hundred miles northeast of here."

Maddy looked skeptical. "You think Vikings carved these markings inside the well?"

"I doubt this well is that old. The Kensington Runestone dates back to 1362."

"Looks pretty old to me," muttered Lizzie.

"Maybe whoever dug this well picked up some runestones along with the other rocks when they built this wall," said Bootsie.

"Where did Mad Matilda get the markings on her quilt?" asked Aggie. Trying to piece it all together, without much luck.

"Maybe she copied them off these rocks," said

Lizzie. Like Occam's Razor, always looking for the simplest explanation.

"We're all guessing," Cookie pointed out. "Let's wait to see what Daniel Sokolowski's expert has to say."

≈ ≈ ≈

Daniel Sokowloski rubbed his gray-streaked beard with one hand, as if petting a cat, while he thumbed through an old-fashioned carousel-style Rolodex with the other. "Here it is," he said. "Ezra Pudhomme. He's an expert on Runology. You may be familiar with his biography of Friedrich Bernhard Marby, the noted rune occultist."

"Must have missed that one," said Maddy.

Cookie spoke up. "Wasn't Marby the Germanic neopaganist who developed a set of occult exercises he called runic gymnastics?"

"Yes, the exercises were used as a means of channeling runic power. Or at least that was Marby's theory." Sokolowski grinned like a Cheshire cat, delighted to have found someone who shared his esoteric trivia.

"So where is this Ezra Pudhomme located?" asked Bootsie, eager to get them back on a subject she understood. Runic power – what the heck was that?

"Ah, it seems you ladies are in luck," said Sokolowski. "Professor Pudhomme happens to be doing a lecture series at ISU this semester."

"In Indy?" asked Lizzie. Her son Josh went to school there.

"Yes. A visiting professorship."

"Will you introduce us?" asked Maddy. "We could drive down for lunch tomorrow."

"Hold on and I'll phone him right now."

"Oh boy, a trip to Indianapolis," said Aggie.

"You'll have to ask your mother," her grandmother warned.

"What about N'yen? Can he come along? He's feeling left out."

Maddy was about to say he'd have to ask his mother, but caught herself. Kathy was still in the hospital – in traction, for goodness sake. N'yen was her responsibility for the next two weeks. "Alright, the two of you can come along," she acceded.

≈ ≈ ≈

Mayor Beauregard Hollingsworth Madison IV was unhappy about the meeting he'd had that morning with that pushy SBI agent. Lt. Neil Wannamaker was much too aggressive for Beau's taste. How dare he insinuate that one of Beau's office visitors might be a cat burglar capable of stealing the Wilkins Witch Quilt. All 13 names in his appointment book were leading citizens, the *crème de la crème* of Caruthers Corners society you might say. Not a shady character among them.

"Becky," he called to his secretary, "cancel my afternoon appointments. I'm going home. My stomach's acting up." In a small town like this, the term "administrative assistant" had not yet caught on.

"Okeydokey," she replied. All but snapping her chewing gun. Becky Marsch was fresh out of high school. This was her first job, according to the application. Beau wasn't sure she was going to work out. The girl daydreamed too much.

He wandered across the town square, pausing to watch the Poindexter twins play catch. Looked like Larry had a new catcher's mitt, while Lonny seemed content with his old glove.

As he turned onto Melon Pickers Row, the sidewalk got wider. One of the perks of having Public Works report to him. The street was lined with maple trees, tall and leafy. In autumn it looked as if the entire block was ablaze.

He noticed a black SUV, a Toyota, parked in

his driveway. That was strange. Maddy was off with her Quilters Club cronies, so who would be at his house. Burglars didn't usually operate in broad daylight, he assured himself.

"Hello!" a tall man in a loose-fitting dark suit hailed Beau as he approached. The man had been standing behind the big leafy witch-hazel in the yard, having himself a smoke.

"Can I help you?"

"My card," the man brandished a sliver of paper that announced: *Maury Seiderman, Field Investigator, G.M.O.P.A.*

Beau stared at the card. "What's G.M.O.P.A.?" he said.

The man gave him a crooked smile. His face was thin, his eyebrows hooding purplish eyes (color contacts?), and he sported a pencil-thin moustache like a Lounge Lizard or silent movie star. "Greater Midwest Occult Phenomena Association. We're a non-profit organization out of Chicago."

"Never heard of it."

"We're an under-the-radar organization. Not seeking publicity."

Beau sized up the visitor. A beanpole, kids might've called him. Over 6' 5" but barely breaking 120 pounds. Even taller than Beau. "Tell me how I can help you. We've got all the magazine subscriptions we need."

"Oh, we only publish a newsletter. And it's free to members."

"Well, my wife and me, we're not the joining type either."

The weird smile flickered, and then became fixed, like the face on a wax mannequin. "We're not recruiting right now."

"Then what do you want?"

"I'm here on official G.M.O.P.A. business. It has to do with that witch's quilt you lost."

Chapter Seven

Worrying About a Witch

Maddy Madison prepared duck a la orange with dirty mashed potatoes, glazed carrots, and an arugula salad with watermelon dressing for dinner. N'yen's favorite. She was making up to the boy for leaving him in the care of Aggie's mother today. He was still pouty.

Beau piled a mound of potatoes onto N'yen's plate. The two had grown close. "Eat up, young man. You want to grow as tall as Grampy, don't you?"

Beau Madison was well over 6', a James Cromwell type. N'yen looked up at his grandfather with a twinkle in his brown eyes. "Not likely. We *Kinh* are usually short."

Aggie looked up. "What's a *Kinh*?"

"That's the kind of Vietnamese I am. I was born in Chicago, but my first parents came from the *người Kinh.*"

"Do you remember your ... first parents?" Maddy asked.

"No, I was little when they died in a car crash. Now my new family has been in a car crash too."

"Your mommy and daddy are going to be all right. They broke some bones, but those will mend."

"You promise?"

"Yes, I do."

"Good. I like my new family."

"That's my boy," said Beau. A Viet Nam vet, he'd been reluctant to accept the boy at first. But that went out the window once the two met. Now they were fishing buddies, often accompanying Lizzie Ridenour's husband Edgar on hook-and-line forays along the Wabash.

"Want to go to Indianapolis tomorrow?" asked Maddy. "The Quilters Club is going to meet a man who might be able to read that writing on the quilt. You and Aggie can come along for the ride, if you like."

"Oh boy, we're going to play detective!"

Beau shook his head, the wispy white hair

stirring with the effort. "Don't encourage this fantasy that you're the No. 1 Ladies Detective Agency."

"And why not?"

"Because you're not. You're a quilting society with nosey members."

"Same thing," said Maddy, nose in the air.

Beau rolled his blue eyes. "Heaven help me," he sighed.

About then, their son Freddie and his wife Amanda dropped by. "Is it too late for desert?" grinned Freddie. He was very fond of watermelon pie.

"Pull up a chair," said Maddy. "We are just about to cut the pie. But this is your sister Tilly's recipe, so it has strawberries mixed in."

"Strawberry-watermelon pie?" said Amanda. "That sounds interesting." She was followed into the dining room by their adopted daughter Donna Ann, the latest addition to the Madison clan (not counting Tilly's newest baby).

"I did say it was Tilly's recipe, didn't I?" Maddy grinned. Tilly was not known as a cook. "But I promise you'll like it."

"Whose black Toyota was parked in the driveway this afternoon?" asked Freddie. "I drove by on my way to clown practice." After being horribly scarred in an Atlanta fire, he'd returned to Caruthers Corners with his family to become a clown who entertained children at the Haney Bros. Zoo and Exotic Animal Refuge on the outskirts of town. The greasepaint may have covered his disfigured face, but it didn't disguise his pleasure in entertaining the local kids.

"A car in our driveway?" repeated Maddy.

"Well, I was going to mention that," said Beauregard Madison. "Just hadn't got around to it."

"Was it anybody we know, dad?" pressed Freddie. "I didn't recognize the car."

"No, no. It was just some quack. A field investigator for some witch-hunters organization. A real kook."

"Witch hunters?" said Aggie. "Is he hunting for Mad Matilda?"

"H-has she come back to haunt people?" stuttered N'yen. The Vietnamese boy fervently believed in witches and spirits of the dead. In Asia they were known as *vong hồn, oan hồn,* or *bách linh.*

"Beau, you're frightening the children," chastised his wife.

"No, he's not," protested Aggie.

"I'm not afraid of no ghosts," parroted N'yen. But there was a quaver in his voice. He still thought *Ghost Busters* was a horror film.

Beau Madison motioned everyone to calm down. "Take it easy," he said. "There's no ghost of Mad Matilda running around Caruthers Corners. Just this guy from the Greater Midwest Occult Phenomena Association looking for information about the missing quilt."

"What kind of information?" Maddy wanted to know. Her suspicions were easily aroused.

"Something about those symbols around the border of the quilt being a prophecy. Or a curse. Or something like that."

"A prophecy?" said Aggie. "What's that?"

"A prediction of the future," her Aunt Amanda offered. "But nobody can really predict the future."

Freddie laughed. "What about your Uncle Bernie? He's correctly predicted the Super Bowl winner for the last ten years."

"We don't talk about Uncle Bernie – he's a bookie. He handicaps sporting events based on stats and such. Nothing occult about that."

Maddy sliced the pie and served it on her

special Blue Willow desert plates. She added a scoop of vanilla ice cream as she passed the pie around the table. "What kind of prophecy" she asked her husband.

"Didn't say. The guy was nuts. You could tell that just by looking at him. He could've been a character out of *Plan 9 From Outer Space*."

Amanda looked up from her strawberry-watermelon pie. "Isn't that supposed to be one of the worst movies ever made?"

"My point exactly," said Beau. "The guy was downright creepy."

"I've seen that movie," grinned N'yen. "There's a zombie and a vampire and invaders from another planet."

"Thank goodness we only have a witch to worry about," said Maddy, giving the boy another slice of pie.

Chapter Eight

The Visiting Professor of Runology

The drive to Indianapolis was uneventful. They only had to stop twice for N'yen to pee. Once at a service station, another time at a McDonald's. Ronald was still serving breakfast, so everybody but Bootsie had an Egg McMuffin; she ordered the oatmeal. This week she was dieting.

Visiting professor Ezra Pudhomme, the expert on Runology, met them at his on-campus office. He was a fat man, a human Jabba the Hutt. At a quick guess, he probably weighed in at 400 pounds. Two metal canes helped him waddle to his desk, where he deposited his bulk onto a couch that served as his office chair. "What's this question you have about runes?" he wheezed. "Dan Sokolowski didn't give me many details."

Cookie Bentley laid the color photograph of the Wilkins Witch Quilt onto the professor's desk blotter. "Are the symbols around the quilt's border runes or some other half-forgotten language?" she got straight to the point.

"Ahem, runes are *not* a language *per se*. They are a form of writing developed by Germanic people before the adoption of the Latin alphabet." You'd think he was teaching Communications History 101, one of his more popular freshman courses. "These are indeed runes, the Scandinavian variant known as *Futhark*. The name comes from the first six letters in that alphabet – *Fehu, Uruz, Thurs, Ansuz, Ræið*, and *Kaun*. The symbols originally meant wealth, water, giant, god, journey, and fatal disease."

"That's fascinating," said Bootsie, barely able to hide her sarcasm. "But what has that to do with the price of ice in Iceland?"

Ezra Pudhomme sniffed haughtily, but refused to acknowledge her snide remark. "If you look at the photograph of your quilt, you will see some of those same runes. I'd say a loose translation might go like this –" He squinted over the image, using a magnifying glass because the inscriptions were small, even in this 8" x 10" color print. "'*After a long journey, we are befallen by a fatal disease, so we hide our wealth in this deep water.*'"

"Wealth?"

"The rune also means cattle, that being a common source of wealth. But here I'd say it refers to some kind of money or treasure."

"Viking money?"

"Vikings did use this form of writing, so possibly."

"What kind of money did the Vikings use?" asked Liz Ridenour, ever the banker's wife. "Paper currency, metal coins, what exactly?"

"The Vikings did sometimes strike coins, but their basic exchange was what we call 'hack silver,' small bars that could be carried and easily cut – or hacked – to the size needed. The Norse did not place a face value on coins. Value was based entirely on the weight of the silver."

Maddy tried to pin the professor down. "So you think this writing around the edge of the quilt is talking about silver bars?"

"Well, yes. But of course, it's meaningless here."

"Meaningless?" huffed Cookie. She would not allow the quilt's authenticity to be challenged. There was an established chain of ownership – provenance, it's called – from Matilda Wilkins to her relative to the Historical Society.

"What I'm saying, the runes on this quilt are

likely decorative, taken from somewhere else. Vikings never would've left a message on a flimsy quilt. They carved their messages onto runestones and other solid structures. Bells, bracelets, horns, buildings."

"This quilt was stitched in 1897," said Cookie. "Where would a turn-of-the-century witch woman learn how to write in – what did you call it? – *Futhark*?"

Pudhomme sat up, his body moving like a geological upheaval. "Witch, you say? That changes things. Perhaps the rune symbols were handed down as an occult tradition. Some people believed runes were not simply letters to spell words, that they also had deeper meanings ... magical or divinatory uses. The word *rune* itself means 'secret, something hidden.' Prior to their use as an alphabet, runes were used for different magical purposes, such as casting lots or casting spells."

Bootsie crossed herself. More out of superstition, for she wasn't even a Catholic. "Heaven help us," she said. "To think this witch's quilt has hung in our Town Hall for over a hundred years."

"Don't be silly," snapped Cookie Bentley. "We

don't believe in witches. Matilda Wilkins was just a crazy old woman who made money selling love potions to hapless farmers – a snake oil salesman at best, a mad hatter at worst, but certainly not a woman with supernatural powers."

"Yes, I guess you're right," Bootsie acquiesced. "But it's downright spooky. We never suspected that those decorative symbols on the quilt contained a secret message."

≈ ≈ ≈

The Indiana State Police's lead investigator Neil Wannamaker had determined that the quilt theft had been pulled off by someone who knew the building's security code, allowing the burglar to escape by resetting it from the inside of the Town Hall after hours. An examination by the alarm company confirmed that someone reset the code at 1:03 a.m.

That hick police chief had pretty much exonerated all the city officials, Wannamaker told himself, but the janitor remained a loose end. Maybe Jasper Beanie didn't do the job himself, but he could have passed the alarm code on to a confederate. After all, Beanie was dirt poor, living in a shabby cottage provided by the Pleasant Glade Cemetery for its caretaker. And he had a history of drunkenness, often spending the night in jail in Burpyville. He drank over there because Caruthers Corners didn't have any bars.

Jasper Beanie was a weak man with financial needs. The perfect motivation for a crime.

Lt. Wannamaker crosschecked Jasper Beanie's telephone records against a list of his former cellmates, looking for any connection with a known criminal. Turns out, Beanie had been in regular contact with a petty shoplifter named Sam Stickley, A/K/A Sam Stickyfingers.

Aha!

≈ ≈ ≈

Liz Ridenour's husband had retired a couple of years ago as bank president. These days, he spent much of his time fishing. His scraggly hair, bushy gray beard, and grubby clothes belied his one-time executive appearance. Gone was the pinstriped suit and power tie, the wing-tipped shoes and $40 haircut. He could have easily passed as a hobo, a man without a penny in his pocket or a care in the world.

Edgar Ridenour was letting his aluminum flatboat drift with the current, his fishing line trolling behind. Fact was, he was snoozing in the afternoon sun, unconcerned that his boat was ten miles downstream from where it was supposed to be. He didn't have any board meetings or bank examiners to worry about. His pension was fully funded, more than enough for an ongoing life of leisure. And fishing.

Edgar came awake when he heard voices above his head. Opening one eye, he noted that he was under a bridge, caught up in a little eddy that kept his boat in place. Maybe it was the word he'd just overheard that caught his attention: *Witch*!

He'd heard enough at home about the Quilters Club looking into the disappearance of that old quilt from the Town Hall. The one supposedly sewn by a witch. So what was this conversation coming from the bridge all about?

"Everybody thought those were some kinda magic symbols on that patchwork monstrosity. Little did they know it was a secret message."

"Secret message?"

"Yeah, like a treasure map. Giving the key to a hidden treasure."

"Ah, c'mon. That old rag has been on display forever. How come nobody ever figured out it was a secret message?"

"Beats me. Guess it was hidden in plain sight. A message in some kinda foreign language nobody here spoke."

"How do *you* know about it then?"

"Some kid figured it out. A *Lord of the Rings* geek. He was visiting the Town Hall with his mama to pay her property taxes when he spotted it."

"*Lord of the Rings*, huh?"

"Yeah, there's been three or four movies, so it has a big following. Like Trekkies with *Star Trek.*"

"So the message is like written in Klingon?"

"No, you idiot. Klingon's a made-up language. This is a real language that elves speak."

"Elves. Now I know you're bonkers. Ain't no such thing as elves and fairies and pixies."

"Well, there's Hobbits. That's a known fact. And they write in this secret language called runes."

"But how did you hear about this secret message?"

"My buddy's connected with the boy's mom. The kid told him. That gave my buddy the idea to steal the quilt."

"Because it's valuable?"

"No, 'cause it can lead to a Viking treasure worth zillions. That ol' witch knew where it's hidden."

"Dang."

"You can say that again, Bud."

"Dang."

Edgar thought he recognized one of the voices.

Chapter Nine

Jasper Beanie's Hard Year

Jasper Beanie was sweating it out in an interrogation room at the State Police office in Indianapolis. There were no windows, so he felt a tad claustrophobic. The State Police's Central District is located in the basement of the Indiana Statehouse, near War Memorial Plaza, a five-city-block memorial built to honor WWI veterans. Only Washington DC has more veterans' monuments than Indy. But Jasper couldn't see any of them from this cramped belowground dungeon.

"We're looking for your accomplice, a guy named Stickley," said Lt. Wannamaker, pointing an accusing finger at his prisoner. The tip was yellow with nicotine. The policeman had developed a three-pack-a-day habit. It was a stressful job, catching crooks.

"Sam Stickley? Yeah, I know 'im, but he ain't no accomplice of mine," grumbled Jasper.

"Admit it," said Wannamaker. "You slipped ol' Stickyfingers the alarm code so he could steal the Wilkins Witch Quilt. How are you two splitting the money – fifty-fifty?"

"Hey, I told you before, that robbery happened on my day off. I wasn't even there. Matter of fact, I was sleeping one off in the Burpyville jail. They'll confirm it. I'm a regular there."

"You think that gives you an alibi? You're just as guilty as Sam Stickyfingers if you gave him the code. It's like one of those contests where you don't have to be present to win."

Jasper Beanie screwed up his face as if about to cry. "You got it all wrong. Sam couldn't have done it either. He was in jail that same night, arrested for shoplifting light bulbs at Home Depot."

"Light bulbs?"

"Said his apartment was too dark. Needed some 100-watt bulbs."

Wannamaker was at a loss for words. If Sam Stickley's alibi held up, he didn't have a suspect.

≈ ≈ ≈

Jasper Beanie had survived a hard year. His

wife Nan had divorced him to run off with the former mayor of Caruthers Corners, an old crook named Henry Caruthers. His great-great grandfather had been one of the town's founding fathers, as had Beau's.

The kick in the pants came when Judge Cramer awarded Nan alimony. So in addition to his job as the cemetery's caretaker, he'd been moonlighting as the Town Hall janitor and as a pool man at the Hoosier State Senior Recreation Center. No wonder he drank, he told himself.

Now this, being accused of stealing the Wilkins Witch Quilt. He'd surely lose his job at the Town Hall over this. Maybe even be ousted from his cottage at the cemetery. This couldn't get any worse.

But it did.

≈ ≈ ≈

Sam "Stickyfingers" Stickley surrendered to the ISP and offered to turn state's evidence implicating Jasper Beanie in return for a suspended sentence. He claimed to know where Beanie had hidden the quilt.

Fact was, both Stickley and Beanie were innocent. But as a career criminal, Stickyfingers was used to playing snitch in return for favors.

Truth be damned, this seemed like a good way to get the coppers off his back. And a good way to get back at Jasper for not loaning him the $50 he'd been phoning him about. He needed the money to buy a bus ticket to Des Moines to visit his daughter. His former cellmate had seemed like an easy touch, but no go. He'd be sorry.

"You're sure about this?" asked Lt. Wannamaker. He wanted to believe Stickyfingers in the worst way, a chance to wrap up this case. But the Burpyville police confirmed that one Samuel L. Stickley had been their guest on that Monday night in question. Hard to get around that.

"I swear on my mother's grave," the crook raised his hand as if taking an oath. "Me and Jasper did it. He has the quilt hidden in a crypt in the cemetery. Do we have a deal?"

"Not so fast. We gotta check it out. In the meantime you can bunk down in our holding cell. You'll find it more comfortable than Burpyville's accommodations."

Burpyville! That's when Sam Stickley realized his confession was going to be proven false. He wondered how much jail time he'd get for that.

≈ ≈ ≈

On the way back from visiting Professor Pudhomme, the Quilters Club was abuzz with new theories.

"I'll bet Mad Matilda belonged to a witches' coven that used runes as magical incantations," posited Bootsie. "Maybe those symbols came over from the Old Country and were passed down through the centuries."

"Matilda's maiden name was Süderdithmarschen," recalled Cookie. This info came from her research in the Historical Society's archive of *Burpyville Gazettes*. "That's a Germanic or Old Norse name."

Bootsie nodded. "Norway, they had witches over there, didn't they?"

"Dunno," shrugged Maddy, eyes on the road. Folks in Caruthers Corners spent more time studying the Bible than Scandinavian folklore.

"No, I don't think it was anything to do with magic," disagreed Lizzie. "I think she used that secret alphabet to mark where she hid a treasure."

"Where would Mad Matilda get a treasure?" argued Bootsie. "Her family had to be dirt poor, living in a tiny stone cottage in the middle of nowhere."

"Legend has it she became wealthy selling

potions," Cookie reminded them.

"No, I mean Viking treasure," said Lizzie. "Silver bars."

"We don't *know* there was a Viking treasure," Maddy pointed out.

"That's what the runes say," insisted Lizzie. Buying into the theory of Norsemen hiding a treasure while camping near the old Wilkins place.

"Good point," Bootsie came around to that way of thinking. "The runes did say there was a treasure. Why would Matilda Wilkins put that message on the quilt if she wasn't leaving a clue?"

Cookie shook her head. "I think it's highly unlikely that an uneducated farmer's wife in the Midwest would know how to read or write an obscure runic alphabet like *Futhark.*"

"Then how did she manage to leave that message if she didn't know what the symbols meant?" argued Lizzie.

"Maybe she didn't know what the symbols meant," Aggie spoke up from the backseat. "What if she simply copied the markings she found inside the well onto her quilt?"

"Inside the well?"

"You said those markings in the well looked like those on the quilt."

"Kinda," said her grandmother. "But we didn't examine them closely."

Aggie gazed out the car window, watching the rolling green countryside slide by. "Like I said, maybe she simply copied the markings she found on those rocks."

"Why would she do that?" said Lizzie. Still not convinced, she was stuck on the treasure map scenario.

"Because they *looked* like magic markings."

"Actually, that makes sense," admitted Cookie. "Copying those runes inside the well without a clue what they meant."

Bootsie wrinkled her brow. "Okay, but how did rocks with Viking writing get inside that well in the first place?"

"There's credible documentation that Norsemen visited America 500 years before Columbus," replied Cookie. "And there's some evidence they made it this far west. The Kensington Runestone, for example. Also nineteen axes, seven halberds, four swords, twelve spears, five steel fire-strikers, and thirty-eight mooring-hole sites. Even rock carvings in Oklahoma have been attributed to Vikings. Who's to say these explorers didn't leave other runestones? Perhaps Mad Matilda's husband used some of them to build a wall around his well. It's not hard to imagine she copied the inscriptions onto her quilt because they looked magical."

Lizzie looked triumphant. "That would imply there's a Viking treasure buried near here – just like I said."

"Maybe there is," said Cookie. "People find pirate treasure all the time in the Caribbean. And sunken ships laden with gold bars and silver coins have been recovered off the Florida Keys. So why not Viking treasure just waiting to be found?"

"Here in Indiana?" scoffed Bootsie. "This is a long way from Norway."

"Maybe so," said Maddy. "But we all saw the markings inside that well."

≈ ≈ ≈

Edgar Ridenour caught the police chief at 5:15 p.m., just as he was punching out to go home. Jim Purdue and his four deputies kept track of their hours with a sputtering old time clock.

"Hold up, Jim," the retired banker called to his friend. "I've got some information you need to hear about."

"Can it wait till tomorrow? I promised Bootsie

I'd be home on time. She's making watermelon stew."

"Hmm, I do love your wife's stew."

"Come home and join us for dinner. She'll have made a big pot of that nectar of the gods."

"Sorry, but I've been fishing all day. Need to get home, take a hot shower. I promised to take Lizzie to that new restaurant in Burpyville – Jack Splat's."

"Isn't that a health food restaurant?"

Edgar removed his baseball cap and ran his hand through his thinning hair. "Lizzie promises if I'll take her there, we can go to Big Bob's Steakhouse this coming weekend. I'm looking forward to chowing down on a 32-ounce Porterhouse, let me tell you that."

"So what's this news that won't keep?"

"You know Boyd Atkins's boy Charlie?"

"Know Boyd better. He was chairman of the Planning Committee for last year's Watermelon Days. I had the dubious pleasure of serving on it with that old tyrant."

"Well, I was out fishing today. My boat drifted under that bridge out on 101. I overheard Charlie Aitkens telling some fellow called Bud that he knew who stole the quilt."

"Probably just big talk."

"I don't think so. They didn't know I was under the bridge. Sounded pretty serious."

"Okay, I'll check it out. But not till in the morning. I'm going home for some of Bootsie's watermelon stew. It's her own recipe y'know."

Chapter Ten

A Picnic at Gruesome Gorge

Maddy got sidetracked again. Her son Bill called to say Kathy had taken a turn for the worse. Her fractured hip had become infected and there was talk of another operation. Maddy knew the couple didn't have any hospitalization insurance and the bills would be piling up. As inner city youth counselors they barely made minimum wage.

Bill's sister Tilly and Mark the Shark decided to drive up. Mark thought he might look into the insurance coverage of the trucking company whose rig had broadsided Bill and Kathy's Subaru.

That meant Maddy would be watching over Aggie and her younger siblings as well as N'yen. With four kids underfoot, it would be like running a Day Care. Quite a few years had passed since she'd cared for Bill, Freddie, and Tilly under one roof.

Thankfully, Freddie's wife Amanda had offered to help out. But that meant adding her daughter to the milieu.

"Don't worry," Beau assured his grandson. "Your mommy will be just fine. Doctors work miracles these days."

"You sure, Grampy?"

"My word of honor." He knew the boy was afraid of being orphaned again. "Your Uncle Mark is going up there to see to it."

"Can I go too? I want to see my mommy."

"Not yet. But soon. Meanwhile, you stay here and I'll take you fishing. I've got a few days of vacation saved up."

"Fishing? Oh boy."

"And your Uncle Freddie promises to take you out to Haney Bros. Circus. He and Sprinkles have worked up a new clown act."

"I like those clowns – even if I know one of them's Uncle Freddie under the makeup."

After being horrible scarred in that fire, Freddie had retired from Atlanta Fire Rescue Department and moved back to Caruthers Corners with his wife. His disability check allowed him to spend most of his time entertaining local kids as Sparkplug the Clown, his disfigurement hidden behind clown makeup.

"Meanwhile, your Uncle Mark and Aunt Tilly will check on your mommy and daddy, make sure they're all right."

"Okay. But I still miss them."

"I know you do," Beau Madison nodded. "I know you do."

≈ ≈ ≈

"I'm so worried," Maddy told her friends. She and her Quilters Club cronies phoned back and forth every morning. "Kathy has been such a good wife for Bill. He'd be devastated if her lost her. We all would."

"This second operation is not life threatening, is it?" asked Lizzie. Always trying to minimize life's worries, the result of a privileged upbringing.

"Supposedly not. But you never know what could go wrong."

"Nothing's going to go wrong. They'll just clean out the infection, pump her full of antibiotics, and send her home before you know it. That's the way these things work. I have a cousin who had a toenail infection —"

"Liz Ridenour, don't tell me that story. Your cousin lost her toe."

"Only one. She has nine others."

Bootsie was more sympathetic. "Little N'yen has really bonded with Kathy. I know he's worried about his mom."

The adopted Vietnamese boy had been with his new home for about a year, but other than his differing skin tone you would have thought he was born into it. His biological parents had survived the Vietnam War, only to come to America and have a bus hit their Honda Civic. N'yen was the only survivor of the crash, fastened safely in his car seat in the backseat. His folk and the drunken bus driver died. Fortunately, it had been 2 o'clock in the morning and the bus was empty, heading back to the garage. Windy City Transport's insurance company paid out two million – one mil per parent – to the orphaned infant. The money was tucked away in a college fund. But he'd spent nine years in foster homes before Bill and Kathy came along.

Cookie came through in a more practical way. With all the children under Maddy's care, she organized a day at Gruesome Gorge. Despite its name, Gruesome Gorge was a wonderful state park with a campground, hiking trails, and a waterfall that flowed into a lovely oval-shaped pond. There on the small sandy beach the Quilters Club had a picnic with the menagerie of kids. Aggie and N'yen splashed about under Bootsie's supervision in Bottomless Pond. (Contrary to its dread description, the pond was no deeper than three feet at any given point.)

"This was a good idea," Maddy told her friend Cookie. "Everybody seems to be having fun." She was cradling her daughter Tilly's youngest in her arms, the infant zonked out after a bottle of warm milk. Lizzie was watching the others.

The sun was bright in a cloudless sky, a perfect day for an outing. The mood belied the park's sordid history, hinted at in its name. Back in the early 1800's, Indian fighters slaughtered a tribe of Potawatomi, trapping them in the gorge like fish in a barrel. No one wrote of this shameful episode in the history books, merely implying that settlers pushed the indigenous natives off their lands.

The state's name actually means "Indian Land," an appellation that dates back to the 1760s. Then in 1800 Congress officially incorporated Indiana Territory, setting it off from the Northwest Territory.

Picnickers sometimes found arrowheads and pottery shards on the grounds of Gruesome Gorge, the only remnants of the Potawatomi. The 1838 removal of the Potawatomi in northern Indiana to designated areas west of the Mississippi was known as the "Trail of Death" (not to be confused with the Cherokee's "Trail of Tears" – although both were carried out under the Indian Removal Act signed into law by President Andrew Jackson).

"We need to go back to Mad Matilda's cottage and check out those runes in the well," Cookie was saying.

"Not really," argued Maddy. "The old woman copied them onto her quilt, and we have a picture of the quilt. Professor Pudhomme gave us a good enough translation. We know all that we're going to know about the location of the treasure."

"An excursion of thirty Norsemen could have carried quite a lot of silver. It would be a valuable find."

"More valuable than a hundred thousand dollar quilt?"

"Oh yes. Millions maybe."

"But anyone who knew runology could have translated the message without having to steal the quilt."

Cookie laughed. "True. But what a clever double crime, the thief got the quilt ·*and* the treasure map in one fell swoop."

Lizzie wandered over to join Maddy and Cookie in the shade of a leafy elm tree. "According to Edgar's story," she interjected, "it was a *Lord of the Rings* fan who spotted the runes. His mother's boyfriend stole it."

"Who do we know that's dating a single mom?" Bootsie called from the water's edge. Sound carried in this boxy canyon.

Maddy turned in her direction. "Good question. But we'll find out. The guy Edgar overheard was Boyd Atkins's son, Charlie. I imagine your husband is calling on him at this very moment to find out his buddy's name."

"Yes," said Bootsie. Her short dark hair was plastered against her head from standing under the waterfall. She looked like a plump little sausage in her black one-piece swimsuit. "I predict we'll have that quilt back on the wall of the Town Hall by the end of the week."

"Wouldn't that be nice," sighed Cookie. As secretary of the Historical Society, she felt responsible for the quilt.

"Don't worry," said little Aggie. "The Quilters Club will find it."

≈ ≈ ≈

Police Chief Jim Purdue and his deputy drove out to Aitkens Produce to interview Charlie. This was a delicate matter, considering his father was the biggest landholder in the county. The farmer pulled a lot of weight on the town council.

The main house reminded you of South Fork, that stately edifice you see on the opening credits of *Dallas*. Over to the west was a gigantic watermelon warehouse, a steel-framed building as big as a city block. Positioned between them was a two-story red barn. A blue Ram pickup was parked in front of the open barn door. The vanity plate – **Aitkens 3** – identified it as Charlie's. Boyd was **Aitkens 1** and his oldest boy Ralph was **Aitkens 2.**

Jim Purdue pulled his squad car next to the pickup. He wondered if Charlie might be inside the barn. "Let's peek inside before we try the house," he suggested to his deputy.

Pete Hitzer nodded as he unholstered his Glock.

"Hey," said Jim, "you're not going to need that."

"Don't be too sure. I know Charlie Aiken. Went to high school with him. He's a hothead. Got a mean streak."

"Keep it holstered."

"Yes, chief."

The interior of the barn was dark. Jim didn't like standing there silhouetted in the open door. Pete had spooked him, no doubt. "Hello," he called. "Anybody in here? It's Police Chief Jim Purdue."

No answer.

"Hello," he repeated.

Same lack of response.

"Must be over at the house," said Pete.

"Wait. Find a light switch." He had a feeling.

Click!

The barn was flooded with bluish light. There in the center of the floor was a body sprawled facedown. Jim Purdue recognized it as the Aitkens boy.

Talk about a dead end. Without Charlie Aitkens, they'd never be able to identify his buddy who stole the Witch Quilt.

"Looks like somebody konked him in the head with this rock." Pete Hitzer pointed to a fragment of stone laying on the dirt floor beside the body.

"Nothing we can do here. Charlie's dead as road kill. Let's see if any suspects are home."

"Gee, Jim. I've never worked a murder before."

"We don't get many of them around here," the police chief acknowledged. "I've not worked many myself."

Pete picked up the murder weapon, unmindful of fingerprints. But it was unlikely the limestone fragment would hold a latent print anyway. "Lookit this," the deputy said. "Some kind of chicken scratches on this rock."

Jim leaned forward to squint at the angular stone. Sort of a trapezoid shape, like it had been broken off a larger chunk. There were markings on it, sort of like stick figures. Where had he seen that before? Then it came to him: These were like the decorative border on the Witch Quilt.

How did these markings get on a rock used to kill Charlie Aitkens?

Chapter Eleven

Cookie in the Witching Well

On the way back home from their picnic, Maddy and her entourage stopped off at Mad Matilda's cottage. Well, the ruins of the old farmplace. With all the kids under wing, there were two cars – Maddy's SUV and Amanda's hatchback. Maddy's car led the way down the narrow dirt road that dead-ended at the oasis of oak trees.

"There's the well with the funny rocks," Aggie pointed.

"Can I see them?" wheedled N'yen, nose pressed against the car window.

Maddy shook her head. "Too dangerous, young man. The writing's inside the well. If you slipped and fell your mom would be very upset. You're her treasure."

"I thought we're looking for silver treasure,"

said the boy. He was disappointed that he wouldn't get to see the magic writing.

Maddy brought the car to a stop. "Everybody out," she called. "But keep the children away from the well. I'm surprised Boyd Aitkins hasn't had it topped off. An open hole like this could be a legal liability."

The Quilters Club and Aggie stood on one side of the SUV. Amanda and the other children were next to the car in back. "Why did we come back here?" she asked. "This place is kinda spooky, a few trees in the middle of a vast watermelon field. Must've been lonely for Matilda Wilkins out here."

"No doubt," said Lizzie. The redhead was feeling a little uneasy herself.

"Where did they bury Mad Matilda?" Freddie's wife asked.

"They didn't," replied Cookie. "According to the *Gazette* they left her body in the well. Too dangerous to retrieve it, 80-feet down."

"That's no big deal," huffed Bootsie. "They were probably just scared of going down there for a witch's corpse."

"Ooo," said N'yen. "I'm afraid that ol' witch's gonna get me."

"Don't worry, dear," his grandmother assured

him. "Matilda wasn't really a witch. There's no such thing. Just a crazy old lady who fell in the well."

"Got thrown in," Aggie corrected her. "By those bad angels."

"Well, yes, but –"

"Don't sugarcoat it," said Cookie. "Aggie's smarter than the lot of us."

That may have been true. Her recent school test clocked the girl in with an IQ of 160. Genius level, to be sure.

"Got your digital camera?" Cookie addressed the redhead. "And do you have the flashlight?" she turned to Maddy.

"Camera," Lizzie replied, holding up a boxy little Vivitar.

"Flashlight," echoed Maddy, turning it on and off by way of proof. Like the winking of a firefly.

"I've got the rope," Bootsie volunteered, displaying a strand of nylon cord guaranteed at 200 lb. tensile strength.

Cookie set her jaw with grim determination. "Okay," he said, "let's get proof that these are the exact same runes as shown in the photo of the Wilkins Witch Quilt. Lower me down."

≈ ≈ ≈

Later, they would laugh about how Cookie nearly fell in the well. Being the lightest of the Quilters Club members (excluding Aggie), she was the one hanging by a rope over the lip of the well to get a digital shot of the runes. Lizzie says her hand slipped, but Cookie accused her of being worried about breaking a nail. Bootsie grabbed the rope just in time to prevent a disaster. Maddy dropped her flashlight in the well as she struggled to help Bootsie with the rope. Amanda fainted, although she later claimed to have tripped on the damp grass.

The kids thought it was grand fun.

One thing was settled: The comparison between Cookie's digital photo of the well stones and the Historical Society's photograph of the Wilkins Witch Quit was conclusive. Even though the markings on the rocks were hard to see, they clearly matched the quilt markings stroke for stroke.

"Okay," Maddy summed it up. "It's likely Mad Matilda copied the runes on the well stones onto her magical quilt."

"And somebody who could read runes finally saw the quilt and stole it," added Bootsie.

At this point the women were gathered around

the patio table in Maddy's backyard. Amanda was riding herd on the little kids. Aggie and N'yen were sitting with the grownups, having appointed themselves as Quilters Club detectives.

"Couldn't someone have stolen the quilt for itself, not knowing about the secret message on it?" called Amanda from across the yard. Her daughter Donna had managed to turn on the garden hose, squirting one of Tilly's kids.

"No," Bootsie shook her head. "Based on what Lizzie's husband heard the Aitkens boy saying, the quilt *was* stolen because some kid translated the runes."

"That's right," confirmed Lizzie as she refilled her lemonade glass. "Edgar got it straight from the horse's mouth."

"Horse?" asked N'yen.

"Just an expression," his grandmother explained.

"I'd like to have a pony," said N'yen.

"I think you'd have trouble keeping one in your Chicago apartment," laughed his cousin Aggie.

"Uncle Freddie said I could keep a pony at the Haney Bros. Zoo."

"Hey, then I want to get a pony too," rejoined

Aggie.

"Nobody is getting a pony today," shushed Maddy. "They cost too much money."

"Yes, but we can afford ponies after we find that Viking treasure," said Aggie.

"If we find that treasure, all of us can afford ponies," laughed Lizzie as she inspected her nail polish. She *had* chipped one out there at the well.

"First, let's think about who is dating a single mother with a nerdy son," Maddy suggested.

"Why bother," said Bootie. "Jim and his deputy went out this morning to talk with the Aitkens boy. He can tell us who he was talking about."

"That was hours ago. Hasn't Jim told you what he learned?"

"Lordy no. I haven't heard from Jim all day. I've been on a picnic with all of you."

"But you have a cellphone ..."

Bootsie shook her head. "Battery's run down. Forgot to charge it last night."

Lizzie held out her iPhone. "Here, use mine. We're all dying to hear what the Aitkens boy had to say."

≈ ≈ ≈

Beau Madison was the first person the police

chief called after discovering the body of Charlie Aitkens. The second was Lt. Neil Wannamaker of the ISP.

Both had responded with the same word: "Dead?"

"That's right," Jim Purdue had told Wanamaker. "Head bashed in. Big rock laying nearby covered in blood and hair, clearly the murder weapon."

"Any witnesses?"

"Nobody has turned up. Boy's father was over in Burpyville buying a new Peterbilt to haul his watermelon crop. Hired hands were in the field. Charlie's bother Ralph is the foreman. He was out there supervising the pickers."

"Nobody else at the farmhouse?"

"Boyd's wife died about ten years ago. They have an Amish woman who keeps house, cleans and cooks, but this was her day off."

"Well, I can tell you Jasper Beanie and his pal Sam Stickley didn't do it. We've had them in lockup since yesterday."

Chief Purdue cleared his throat. "I could've told you ol' Jasper didn't have anything to do with this. He hasn't got the gumption to steal a paperclip. Beau Madison only keeps him on as janitor at the Town Hall out of pity. His wife used to be Beau's secretary before she ran off with the former mayor."

"Henry Caruthers? We've got a file on him six-inches thick."

"There you have it. Point is, we don't have a suspect."

"Sure we do," Wannamaker contradicted him. "The guy Edgar Ridenour overheard Charlie Aitkens talking about. The one he said stole the quilt. Probably killed the boy to shut him up."

Jim Purdue was frustrated. His hand gripped the phone as if he were choking it. "Yeah, but how are we gonna find that guy?"

"Figure out who Charlie Aitkens was talking to on the bridge and ask him."

"Isn't that your job? You're the state's lead investigator."

"Don't like to step on local toes."

"You don't say?" Was he being set up to take blame for a failed investigation? Those state boys were tricky like that.

Lt. Wannamaker wrapped it up. "I'll check in tomorrow and see how you're doing with your murder investigation. We'll keep looking for the quilt."

"Hey, aren't they the same case?" said Jim Purdue. But the phone clicked in chief Purdue's ear. Conversation ended.

≈ ≈ ≈

Beau Madison had already heard from Boyd Aitkens. Distraught over the death of his son, the powerful landowner wanted assurances that the villain who murdered Charlie would be brought to justice. Lynching's probably what ol' Boyd had in mind, but he had the smarts not to say it out loud.

"Beau, I backed you in your election campaigns. If you want to serve another term, you'd better kick Jim Purdue in the butt and get him to find the murderer. Somebody's gonna pay for this."

"Sorry about your boy, Boyd. He was a good kid. I feel for your loss."

The farmer's weathered face looked as sad as Iron Eyes Cody. "Who would've done such a thing? Charlie didn't have an enemy in the world. He was a little lazy, not a go-getter like his older brother. But everybody liked him, what you'd call a hail-fellow-well-met."

"Chief Purdue thinks it may have been the person who stole the Wilkins Witch Quilt. Edgar Ridenour overhead Charlie telling somebody that he knew who did it. Jim thinks the thief may have killed Charlie to shut him up."

"What would he know about that mangy old quilt? He never paid it no mind."

"Don't know. But you can be sure Jim will find out."

"Forget the police. Jim Purdue has got more experience directing traffic than solving murders. Put your wife on the case."

"M-my wife?"

"C'mon, Beau. Everybody knows that her so-called Quilters Club is like an unofficial private detective agency."

"Whoa, hold on there, Boyd. You've got that all wrong –"

The watermelon farmer stood up, cutting off the conversation. "Let me put it this way, Beau. You get them gals to find the murderer of my son and I'll pony up a hundred grand toward your next election. Use it for radio advertising or take a vacation to Cancun, I don't care which."

Chapter Twelve

Witchcraft in the Midwest

In the late 1600s New England was apparently infested with witches – as exemplified by the notorious Salem Witch Trials. And in the 1800s witching covens were scattered across the South, particularly around New Orleans (mostly Vodou cults). However, in the Midwest the history of witchcraft is scant.

Deep in the bowels of the Indiana State University Library Cookie Bentley had found a rare volume titled *Occult Practices Among Early Settlers of Indiana and Illinois*. This had been a Master's Thesis by a long-forgotten student named Thaddeus Elmer Wapner.

"According to Wapner," Cookie told her comrades, "in 1882 a Master Warlock named Reginald Wentworth Evers settled near Burpyville. He was supposedly an outcast of

Salem, Massachusetts, although records do not support this claim – nor does the timing. He established a small coven of eleven members who met on the full moon of each month. One of these was a woman named Elmira Süderdithmarschen."

"Mad Matilda's mother?"

"Exactly."

"So Matilda Wilkins learned witchcraft at her mother's knee."

"Apparently so."

Bootsie frowned. "Does that mean Matilda Süderdithmarschen Wilkins wasn't mad?"

"Who knows? But she came by her trade of selling love potions and spells honestly," said Cookie. "It was the family business."

"What does that tell us?" sighed Lizzie Ridenour. She was growing impatient with all this old history malarkey. Unlike her friend Cookie, Liz liked to live in the present. No dusty old books and yellowed newspaper clippings for her. She owned a Kindle, for goodness sakes! All the better to read the latest Nora Roberts on.

"Maybe it tells us nothing," Cookie admitted. "Other than that the woman who stitched the missing quilt believed in witchcraft."

"Yes, but did she know about the treasure or

simply copy off those runes from the stones in her well?" pressed Lizzie.

"I think we should look into those Vikings," said little Aggie Tidemore, speaking with childlike insight. "It's their message on that witchy quilt. And they're the ones who hid the treasure."

Bootsie couldn't help but laugh. "Out of the mouth of babes," she said.

"Hey, I'm not a baby," she protested. "I'll be twelve soon!"

"Hm," Cookie thought it over. "I think Aggie might just be on the right trail."

"How do we investigate a group of people that even the archeologists can't prove where here?" grumbled Lizzie.

"Oh, we know they were here," said Maddy.

"How so?"

"Because we've seen their runestones in that old well."

≈ ≈ ≈

Lt. Neil "The Nail" Wannamaker may have told Chief Purdue to take over the Charlie Aitkens case, but he had his own men looking into it too. He sensed the murder was somehow connected to that missing quilt. Who would've thought an old rag like that could be worth a hundred G's?

The first clue his investigator picked up had to do with Charlie's circle of friends. His best pal was a guy named Tommy "Spud" Bodkins, an old football teammate from high school. That was probably who the fisherman – a retired banker – had overheard him speaking with on the bridge. Spud instead of Bud. According to Spud's mother, the two young men sometimes fished off that particular span of concrete and steel, convinced that there was a good catfish hole under it ... but they never caught much.

Unfortunately, Spud had gone off to Indy for the weekend to catch a Colts game. No one knew where he was staying, so Lt. Wannamaker issued an APB for a 5' 2" redhead with a potato-shaped birthmark on his left arm. Shouldn't be too hard to spot a guy of that description, he told himself.

He wondered if the birthmark was the source of Spud's country-bumpkin nickname?

≈ ≈ ≈

Maddy's son-in-law Mark the Shark phoned to say Bill and Kathy were on the mend. Bill was up and about; Kathy's infection had been stemmed with antibiotics. Little N'yen would be seeing his mommy and daddy soon.

While there, Mark had worked out a

settlement with the trucking company. Bill and Kathy's medical expenses would be entirely covered. There was another $200,000 thrown in to cover their "inconvenience." That was quite a windfall for a couple of youth counselors who worked for an underfunded non-profit NGO.

Maddy's youngest son Freddie – A/K/A Sparkplug the Clown –decided to drive up to Wisconsin with his wife and daughter to check on brother Bill too. Maybe he'd put on a little show for the hospital's children's ward while he was up there. He liked his new job of entertaining kids as a member of the Haney Bros. Zoo and Exotic Animal Refuge.

"I was so worried about Bill and Kathy," Maddy told her husband that night after dinner. The grandchildren were in bed or she wouldn't have been so open about her concerns. Some people thought the Law of the Jungle was "Survival of the Fittest," but Maddy knew it was "Don't Scare the Animals." And these were cute little bunnies indeed.

Agnes and N'yen were her two favorite grandchildren, though she would never admit that out loud. Tilly's little ones – Taylor and Madison – were both too little to bond with. And Freddie's daughter Donna was just turning three. Besides, Aggie and her Vietnamese cousin were unofficial members of the Quilters Club. What's more, Aggie was getting quite good at stitching quilting squares!

"Bill and Kathy are going to be just fine," Beau assured his wife. "That's what Mark said. And that boy's never wrong. He gets his facts right. That's what makes him such a good lawyer."

"That and his pit-bull personality. Once he clamps down, he never lets go."

"Determined, that he is."

Maddy leaned her head against her husband's boney shoulder. "I'm so glad he and Tilly worked through that bad patch a few years back."

"Me too. If they hadn't we'd be two grandchildren short."

"And they wouldn't be living a few blocks away from us here in Caruthers Corners." Mark and Tilly had bought the old Taylor House on the town square where Maddy had grown up. She was pleased that her old homeplace was staying in the family.

"Tilly and Freddie have returned to Caruthers Corners," she said. "I wish Bill would come home too."

"Maybe with that settlement Mark worked out with the trucking company, they can afford to quit their jobs and move back," speculated Beau.

"Not likely," said his wife. "Bill and Kathy are determined to save the world. And there's more of the world in Chicago than here in this flyspeck of a town."

"Hey, Caruthers Corners is a nice town," protested Beau, the mayor in him coming out.

"I know, dear. You and I have lived here all our life. There's nowhere else I'd want to be."

"Then Bill and Kathy –"

"– those two kids have lives of their own. They like Chicago. There are plenty of kids who need their help up there."

"Yeah, I suppose so."

"But we can still miss them," his wife said, patting him reassuringly on the arm. "That's allowed."

"Want to watch some television 'fore we turn in?" asked Beau. He liked to have a "little evening" before bedtime. Mindless TV was just the ticket, although he usually slept through the program. "A warm-up for a good night's sleep," he called it.

"That would be nice," nodded Maddy. "Maybe there's something interesting on the National

Geographic Channel."

There was.

They tuned in just in time to catch a program titled *Severed Ways: The Norse Discovery of America*. The dramatization followed two Norse men struggling to survive in the wilds of North America when abandoned by the rest of their expedition.

Afterwards, there was an interview with filmmaker Tony Stone, where he explained what got him interested in these early explorers. "I wanted to know more about it when I heard brief mention of it back in the third grade. I wanted to know more about the Viking conquest in our own backyard … "

Beau's snores were a soft rumble, but Maddy was leaning toward the TV, her senses on high alert. This was fascinating. Maybe there was more to this idea of Vikings reaching Indiana than traditional archeologists thought.

"The Norse site at L'Anse Aux Meadows in Newfoundland was discovered by sailing the geographical description written in the Vinland Sagas, which was Liefsbudir, the base camp Lief Ericson constructed around the year 1000," the filmmaker was saying. "Many of stories in the

Sagas tell of other expeditions that set sail south from there and one expedition describes spending a winter at a location where it did not snow. They could have explored as far south as Virginia or beyond."

Severed Ways posited that a couple of scouts had been left behind during one of the Vikings' battles with "the Skraelings," as they called the North American Indians.

"Most historians agree that they probably traveled into the St. Lawrence and down the American coast," continued the filmmaker. "There just hasn't been any concrete evidence found yet. And it might never. Any archeological site has probably been trampled and plowed on the American coast. It's such a populated region. Plows or other modern machines probably have torn up any fire pit or building footprint that might remain. But you never know what we might stumble upon."

Like a stone well.

Chapter Thirteen

Runestone of Death

Bootsie Purdue was having breakfast with her hubby Jim before he went to work. It was a longtime ritual, a little one-on-one time, because the work of a law officer doesn't always conform to a 9-to-5 routine.

She'd just poured the watermelon juice, when he said, "I've gotta go down to Indy today and pick up Jasper Beanie. He doesn't have a ride home." Jim preferred watermelon juice over orange juice, a hometown foible. After all, Caruthers Corners was known as "the Watermelon Capital of Indiana."

"Now you're a taxi service?"

"I feel obligated. Jasper's being falsely accused has disrupted his life, which wasn't all that good to begin with."

Bootsie tasted her eggs, a little soft for her

liking. She'd been distracted lately with that missing quilt. Her cooking was suffering. "Is Jasper going to lose his job at the cemetery? That would make him homeless."

"No, Beau stepped in there. Told the town commissioners that Jasper was going to continue as caretaker at Pleasant Glade as well as keep his job at the Town Hall."

"Poor Jasper Beanie. He reminds me of that character in the *Li'l Abner* comic strip, the man with the perpetual storm cloud over his head."

"Joe Btfsplk."

"What?"

"Joe Btfsplk, that was the character's name." He pronounced it *Buf-spilk.*

"Oh, right."

"Jasper was always a loser, even in high school," he sighed. "When his wife ran off with Henry Caruthers, that was the final blow to his self-esteem. No wonder he drinks. That's why my deputies are instructed to take him home rather than arrest him when they catch him tying one on in the town square."

"I remember him in high school. He was the waterboy for the football team."

"Yeah, he tried out as a player, but didn't make

the grade."

Bootsie sighed, remembering those halcyon days of their youth. "You and Beau and Edgar were the school's star athletes. You the star quarterback. Beau the winning scorer on the basketball team. Edgar still holder of the 100-yard dash record. Ben Bentley the wrestling champ. All of you on the baseball team the year it won the district series."

"And ol' Jasper always on the sidelines."

"This quilt theft is troubling you, isn't it?"

"Some. But it's Charlie Atkins's murder that has me losing sleep."

"Yes, you tossed and turned all last night."

Jim Purdue rubbed his balding dome. "I'm getting pressure on both sides. The state boys are giving me a hard time. And Charlie's father thinks I'm incompetent. Wants Beau to turn the investigation over to the Quilters Club."

Bootsie almost spilled her watermelon juice. "To us? We're just a handful of busybodies who do needlework."

"You gals have developed quite a reputation as crime-solvers." He stood up and reached for his billed cap with a gold star that said CHIEF. He didn't feel much like a chief today. All told, he felt more kinship with Jasper Beanie than he'd care to admit. "Gotta go. A meeting with that jerk Wannamaker to report our lack of progress."

"He's that ISP lieutenant?"

"Yeah, the one they call The Nail. And with good reason. Every time I meet with him I feel like somebody has driven a sharp object straight into my brain."

"You have been taking a lot of aspirin lately." She'd noticed. Wives do that.

"He wants us to turn over any forensic evidence we have in the Aitkens case. But what kind of clues are you going to find on a rock."

"A rock?"

"That's right. The boy died of blunt force trauma. Somebody coldcocked him with a rock covered in marks."

That got his wife's attention. "What kind of marks?"

"Inscriptions. Engravings. Don't know what you'd call 'em. Probably a chunk that broke off a tombstone. I've assigned a deputy to go over to the cemetery and look for a broken grave marker."

"Were there letters? Words?"

"Naw. Just hen scratchings."

"Can I see it?"

"Hon, it's locked up in the safe down at the station. And Wannamaker's picking it up first thing this morning. Don't tell me the Quilters Club is actually going to poke into my murder investigation? Are you trying to put me outta work?"

She stood on her tiptoes to plant a kiss on his cheek. They were a cute couple, a middle-aged Mutt and Jeff, each maybe twenty pounds overweight, a foot difference in height. "There, there, dear. I was just curious."

"Well, if you really want to see it, there's a photo of the murder weapon over there in my briefcase. Just picked up the pictures from the crime scene yesterday on the way home from work. Bob Tippey over at the *Burpyville Gazette* develops them on the side. Doesn't charge anything when I let him use one in the paper."

Tippey was a small-town newspaper editor who fancied himself a gonna-break-this-town-wide-open crusading journalist. His father had been editor of the paper before him, and his grandfather before that. A family business since the 1800s.

Before Jim Purdue had finished speaking, his wife had pulled the 8" x 10" color photograph from his battered leather briefcase and was examining it with the eyes of an eagle. "Dear, don't waste your deputy's time in the cemetery. This is not a chunk off a tombstone. It's a fragment from a runestone."

≈ ≈ ≈

By noon the Quilters Club was back at the university in Indianapolis, waiting outside the door of visiting professor Ezra Pudhomme. He was running a few minutes late, having just delivered a lecture on Early Sumerian Cuneiform History in Lecture Hall 11-B.

Pudhomme seemed surprised to see them. "Ladies, to what do I owe this unexpected pleasure?" What he really meant was "unannounced visit." He preferred people to make appointments. This summer gig at ISU left his calendar with few free moments. His class load and scheduled lectures were quite arduous.

"Sorry, Professor Pudhomme," apologized Maddy. "We promise to take only a moment of your time. We need you to tell us what these runes say." She held out the color photograph that Jim Purdue had reluctantly let his wife borrow on the grounds she would get it translated for him.

"More runes? Wherever are you getting these?

Did someone come back from a vacation in Scandinavia?"

"No, these are local," interjected Cookie. "We think it's proof of Viking incursions into the Midwest."

"Proof, you say?"

"Even better than the Kensington Runestone."

The fat professor smiled as if appreciating some private joke. "The Kensington Runestone has never truly been authenticated," he said. "Jansson, Moltke, Nielsen, Anderson, and Wahlgren, among others, have asserted that the stone is a forgery."

"What about Hall, Holland, Thalbitzer, and Hagen?" responded Cookie Bentley. "Those experts argued that it's real. And the Smithsonian displayed the Kensington Runestone in 1949, not exactly an institution known for supporting fakes."

"Hm, you've been doing your homework. Very well, let me see your photograph."

Pudhomme pulled out a 3x magnifying glass to help him inspect the image in the photo. His nose hovered inches from the glossy surface as he moved the glass from rune to rune, studying each letter like a Treasury Agent examining a counterfeit twenty.

"Well –?" said Lizzie. Impatient as usual.

"Don't rush me. This is interesting."

"What does it say?" asked Bootsie, antsy to get a translation. She'd promised Jim.

"This is only a fragment, so it is difficult to say. Something about digging a hole –"

"A hole?" said Lizzie, the banker's wife. "You mean like a place to bury treasure?"

"This fragment says nothing about money or treasure."

"But the runes on the Wilkins Witch Quilt mentioned a buried treasure," challenged Bootsie.

"Not exactly," corrected the professor. "The quilt inscription that you showed me contained the rune for *fehu*. That can mean either money or cattle."

"Cattle?" blurted Lizzie. Disappointed that this mystery could be about a herd of cows.

"The fragment in this photo does not contain the symbol *fehu*. Just something about digging a hole."

"You mean like a well?" asked Maddy.

"A water well, buried treasure – who knows?" exclaimed the professor. He was becoming exasperated with these ladies. What did they know of disciplined research and scientific method and responsible translations? Just a small-town coffee klatch sticking their nose where it didn't belong. If this was a photograph of an artifact found locally, it should be the province of archeologists and linguists like himself.

"Thank you for your time," said Maddy, sensing that they had overstayed their welcome. She was disappointed they hadn't learned more. Digging a hole indeed!

"Wait," grunted Professor Pudhomme. "Are you sure the stone in this picture was found in Indiana? That would be a remarkable discovery."

"Who can say," Bootsie interjected. "It was recovered at a crime scene."

"Oh my."

Maddy repeated, "Thanks for your time, professor. We've got to get home in time to fix dinners for our husbands. A housewife's job is never done."

He didn't pick up on her sarcasm.

≈ ≈ ≈

In the car on the way back, the women were trying to sort through the facts as they knew them. This was more difficult than those Sudoku puzzles in the *Indianapolis Star*.

"Fact One," said Maddy, keeping her eyes on the road as she drove. "Somebody stole the Wilkins Witch Quilt."

"And the Indiana State Police have determined it was an inside job," added Lizzie.

"Hey, Jim came to that same conclusion," Bootsie defended her husband.

Maddy didn't see any point of reminding them that her grandson N'yen had been first to put forth that theory.

"Fact Two, we determined that the markings on the quilt were runes, an ancient Norse language," said Cookie. "And that Mad Matilda Wilkins copied those symbols off stones inside her well."

"Fact Three," added Lizzie, "the runes say there's a treasure hidden in a deep hole. Do you think it meant inside the well?"

"It *has* to be down there," said Bootsie. "The message was carved there at the top of a deep hole."

Lizzie continued that line of thought. "And the rock that killed Charlie Aitkens confirms that Vikings dug the well, not Matilda's husband."

Cookie nodded. "A Viking well."

"Now we're getting somewhere," said Maddy.

"We may have located a Viking treasure. Bars of silver at the bottom of the well."

"Don't forget," warned Bootsie, "the bones of Mad Matilda are down there too."

"That's right," said Cookie. "The townspeople left her down there after the Avenging Angels drowned her."

"That's scary," shuddered Aggie in the back seat. "This is like a ghost tale."

"No ghosts," her grandmother assured her. "Just something bad that happened a long time ago."

"So who stole the quilt?" asked Bootsie, still a policeman's wife.

"A guy whose girlfriend has a teenage son," offered Lizzie. "That's what Edgar heard Charlie Aitkens say."

"Oh, that reminds me," said Bootsie. "Boyd Aitkens wants the Quilters Club to find out who killed his son."

Chapter Fourteen

A Well Digger's Nightmare

"**A**re you gals crazy?" shouted Beauregard Madison IV, not a man accustomed to raising his voice. "You want me to send someone down into the Wilkins well based on some cockamamie translation of the markings on a crazy quilt?"

"The markings are inside the well too," said Maddy. At her perky best. Trying to convince her husband. But Beau Madison was known to be as a stubborn as a mule.

"No way," he shook his head firmly. "I'd get laughed out of office, helping the Quilters Club search for a lost treasure."

"Dear, can't you just say a puppy fell in the well and that you're sending out the fire department to rescue it?"

The mayor rolled his eyes. "You're asking me

to lower someone into an eighty-foot well … not retrieve a kitten out of a tree."

"Beau Madison, this is an important piece of Caruthers Corners history," insisted Cookie Bentley. "We have an obligation to check it out." As secretary of the Historical Society, she wasn't going to let a major event like Norsemen visiting Indiana go unexplored.

"Heck, I'll do it," said Ben Bentley.

Cookie turned to her husband. "Do what?"

"Go down in the well. I've helped dig a lot of wells in this county. No big deal."

"You could keep this quiet?" asked Beau, showing a crack in his resistance. He had to live with Maddy. And she seemed determined.

"No biggie," grinned the bearded man. "I'll get a buddy to run the winch. We can do it first thing in the morning. By lunch these girls can be counting their Viking silver."

"Hm, there may be an ownership problem," mulled Beau, rubbing his chin. "That well's on Boyd Aitken's property. Wish Mark the Shark were here to sort this out."

"We have to find some treasure before that becomes an issue," Edgar Ridenour noted. He remained skeptical about Vikings burying silver in the Midwest. But he didn't want to say too much, for Lizzie was all a-twitter about the possibility of finding a cache of silver.

"Good point," grinned Ben.

"I'll call Boyd Aitkens and get his permission," sighed Beau. "Tell him the Historical Society is trying to recover Mad Matilda's bones."

"Perfect," said Maddy.

"Those bones would have a place in our little museum," Cookie nodded. "We'd create a display around them."

They were all seated around the Madisons' dining-room table – Beau and Maddy, Cookie and Ben, Lizzie and Edgar, Bootsie and Jim. The kids were in bed. Aggie would be irked that she'd missed this late-night powwow.

"Now that we've solved the treasure hunting issue, let's talk about who stole the quilt and who killed Charlie Aitkens," said Jim Purdue. "May as well get it out on the table, seeing as Boyd's trying to drag you gals into this."

"We know the same thing as you, dear," said Bootsie. "That Edgar overheard Boyd's son telling someone he knew who stole the quilt."

"That was probably his friend Spud Bodkin," nodded Jim. "At least that's what the state boys tell me."

"Doesn't that make it simple?" said Maddy. "All we have to do is ask Spud who Charlie was talking about."

"Easier said than done," the police chief replied. "Spud's gone missing."

"Missing?" said Edgar.

"That's right. Nobody has seen him in two whole days. Went to Indy to see a Colts game and never came back."

"Maybe he's dead too," suggested Maddy as she poured coffee, refilling everyone's cups. The Madisons liked an inexpensive brand that contained chicory.

"You're saying the thief killed them both to shut them up?"

"That could explain him being missing," she replied.

Lizzie scowled at her coffee cup. She preferred a high-end coffee from Seattle. A Mucho Grande, with two lumps of sugar. "Charlie Aitkens said it was a guy whose girlfriend has a teenage son who's into *Lord of the Rings*. How many people in Caruthers Corners could that be?"

"Hmm," Maddy considered the question. "Mildred Gertner's son Stuart is into *Lord of the*

Rings. She says he's read the book more than a hundred times. Thinks he's a Hobbit or something."

"His ears *are* big and he's barely five feet tall," Lizzie pointed out.

"Hobbits aren't real," snapped Cookie. A woman used to dealing in hard facts, she wasn't attuned to fantasy worlds populated by wizards and dwarfs and fire-demons.

"No ... but that's not the point. The boy's a devotee."

"Mildred can't be the thief's girlfriend," said Bootsie. "She and Frank have been married since high school. No boyfriend in the picture."

"Mildred isn't the woman Charlie was talking about," agreed Maddy. "But her son may know other boys who are hooked on those Tolkien books. I think Jim should question him to see if any of his friends have a single mother with a shifty boyfriend."

"*Ahem*," Beau cleared his throat. "That's not a bad idea, Jim."

The big moon-faced policeman nodded. "I'll put one of my deputies on it first thing in the morning. Got nothing to lose. We don't have any other leads."

Edgar sipped his coffee. He wasn't as fussy about his joe as his wife. Caffeine was caffeine to him. "At least we have a plan of action. Ben goes down in the well tomorrow morning. And Jim starts hunting for Hobbits."

"That about sums it up," said Beau Madison, finishing off his coffee in one gulp. He liked the taste of chicory.

≈ ≈ ≈

Aggie got up to go to the bathroom. It was just down the hall. As she passed her cousin N'yen's room, she heard sobbing.

Tapping on the door, she whispered, "Can I come in?"

"Y-yes," came a tiny quavering voice.

"What's the matter?"

The boy sat up in bed. Aggie could see his silhouette from the moonlight coming through the bedroom window. "I'm worried about my daddy and mommy," he said. "I don't want them to die."

"They're not going to die," the girl reassured him. "They just got banged up a little. That's what my daddy told me, and he never lies. After all, he's a lawyer."

"Honest?"

"Honest Injun. Don't worry so much."

"I'm afraid of being alone again, like after my first mommy and daddy died. They were in a car accident too."

"You won't ever be alone. You've got a family now. Forever."

"Really?"

"Yes, you've got me and grammy and grampy and my daddy and mommy and Uncle Freddie and Aunt Amanda and all your new cousins." She paused. "Besides, your own daddy and mommy will be getting out of the hospital real soon."

"Promise?"

"You know you can always trust me, your very favorite cousin."

≈ ≈ ≈

That same night Jasper Beanie heard a noise outside the caretaker's cottage. Could it be those prankish high-school boys again? They liked to initiate members into the Seniors Scalawag Society by sending unwary boys into the cemetery to retrieve a bone. Some of the crypts were in need of repair, access to skeletons being easier than the town commissioners would care to admit. Principal Dorrety had banned such initiations, but they still went on behind his back.

As Jasper could attest.

Proper procedure was for the caretaker to phone the police and report any trespassers ... but after his week of confinement with the Indiana State Police he wasn't eager to see more lawmen. So he pulled on his trousers and hobbled out the backdoor, flashlight in hand.

"Yo, you boys! Get the heck outta the cemetery. It's closed to the public this time of night."

However, the voce that replied didn't belong to a student at Madison High School. "Hello, Mr. Beanie. Perhaps you could help us? We're looking for a tombstone with a piece broken off."

"There's lotsa tombstones like that. Pleasant Glades is better'n a hundred years old."

"Take a look at the picture," said the voice. "Maybe you'll recognize it as coming from one of your tombstones."

A light flashed on, revealing two men in suits, a photograph held out for him to inspect."

"Just who are you guys?"

"We're with the state police," said Neil the Nail.

Chapter Fifteen

Hunting for Hobbits

Deputy Pete Hitzer interviewed Harry "the Hobbit" Gertner that next morning. Harry's mother gave him permission to call her son out of First Year Algebra for the talk. Harry didn't mind getting out of the math class one little bit. He hated memorizing terms and coefficients. He'd rather be writing fantasy stories in an Elfin language on his online blog.

Principal Dorrety let them use his office. He had sent a teacher's aide to call the boy out of class so as not to upset students with a policeman's presence.

"Fare the well, officer," said the chubby bespectacled nerd. "What wanteth thou of me?" He was dressed in a top hat, vest, and morning coat, despite the school's dress code.

"First off, let's speak the King's English," said

Pete Hitzer. He only had a GED diploma, so he didn't like it when people flaunted their fancy education.

"Alas, these days the Crown is overseen by a Queen. So should we call it the Queen's English?"

The deputy put on his tough face, the one he used when arresting people. "I mean plain ol' American English. Got it, Harry?"

"Uh, yes sir."

"Good. Now here's my question –"

It took three minutes for Deputy Pete Hitzer to get two names of local *Lord of the Rings* aficionados who had single moms.

≈ ≈ ≈

Lt. Neil Wannamaker was on the phone with that hick police chief. "The rock used to kill the Aitkens boy didn't come off a tombstone at Pleasant Glades," he stated as if this were a major revelation.

"Why would you think it did?" replied Jim Purdue, determined not to show his cards.

"Because that's where Charlie's mother is buried. Thought it might have been a keepsake from her grave."

"Sounds pretty ghoulish, taking a piece of his mother's tombstone as a memento."

"Told you it wasn't that. His mother's tombstone is as pristine as the day it was placed there ten years ago."

Jim paused, debating whether to tell him it was a runestone. No, the ISP would never buy that theory. Vikings in Indiana? It was all too crazy. So instead he said, "There are several other cemeteries in the area. Family plots. Small churches. A big one over near Burpyville that's owned by a funeral home chain – Shady Meadows, it's called."

"We've checked them all. I had a dozen men poking around local graveyards yesterday. Went into overtime, up to midnight. That rock didn't come from any of them."

"So where did it come from?"

"Beats me. Maybe it's a souvenir Charlie brought back from Boy Scout camp in Michigan when he was sixteen years old. Maybe its origin isn't even important. But we try to run down every lead."

Jim screwed up his courage. He wasn't used to talking back to the state police. "I thought you said this was my case. What the dickens are your men doing checking out the murder weapon behind my back."

"Just lending a hand. I've got more resources than you do, so why not help you out?"

"Yeah, thanks," Jim said. But he didn't sound sincere.

≈ ≈ ≈

"No," said Cookie to the tall man with the thin moustache, "records of where the Church of Avenging Angels was located do not exist."

"Hey, I checked with the folks at Town Hall. They said to ask you."

"Wish I could help, but the church's location is lost to history. Old newspaper articles suggest it was on the far side of the Never Ending Swamp, but no one knows exactly where. *A Personal History of Caruthers Corners and Surrounding Environs* by Martin J. Caruthers tells us a little about the leader of the church, one Rev. Billingsley Royce. Caruthers claimed the good reverend was really a scalawag from St. Paul, Minnesota, named Billy Bob Rutherford."

"Is he the one who drowned that witch lady?"

"According to reports in an 1899 issue of the *Burpyville Gazette*, a local woman was drowned in her own well by a group of religious zealots. They thought she was a witch – and maybe she thought so too. The men were never identified, but rumor had it that Rev. Royce was the ringleader."

"And nobody ever found the money?"

"W-what money?" Cookie stammered. At this very moment her husband and his pal Bombay were down in the very well where Matilda Wilkins had died. It seemed highly suspect that this stranger would be asking about her murderers on this particular morning.

"Legend has it those religious zealots, as you call them, took Mrs. Wilkins's money and buried it under the doorstep of their church. Silver bars, it was said."

"S-silver bars? Why would an old farmer's wife have silver bars?" She was shocked he knew about the silver.

"Viking treasure she found in her well, the story goes."

"Where did you hear this?" Cookie could feel her hand shaking as she thumbed through the Caruthers book to the paragraph about the witch's death.

"My organization is called the Greater Midwest Occult Phenomena Association. G.M.O.P.A., for short. Or G-Mop-A if you like. We research occult phenomena. We've catalogued over fifty thousand strange happenings since 1800. Naturally, we pay attention to stories about witches. The tale about Rev. Royce and the witch woman's silver appeared in a book called *Angels of the Lord and the Silver Hoard*, supposedly written by one of Rev. Royce's congregation, a man named Simonton Poteet. It was published in 1937 by the Peoria University Press – now defunct."

"If you already know so much about Rev. Royce, why are you quizzing me?" She'd have to get her hands on that book, Cookie told herself.

"We try to be thorough. What's more, we know you and your quilting friends have been poking around the Wilkins homestead. If you're after the silver bars too, you can forget it. I have a deal with Boyd Aitkens, the gent who owns that land."

"Matter of fact, so do we. But I thought you said the money was buried at the church ... or wherever the church used to be located."

"That's just it, we aren't sure. Legends are never totally accurate."

"Yes, I certainly agree."

"Then if you –"

"Sorry, but you'll have to excuse me. I'm behind in my filing."

"I thought you were going to show me the reference in that book. We don't have a copy of it in our library."

"Yes, it's a rare book. In fact, this may be the only copy existent. In 1913 Martin Caruthers paid to have it printed on the *Burbyville Gazette* press. Only 50 copies were pulled, according to the records."

"Does it say more about Rev. Royce?"

"Perhaps. But I'm too busy right now to look it up."

"Hey –"

"Go find the treasure on your own," snapped Cookie, closing the book with a *bang*! "I have work to do."

≈ ≈ ≈

At that very moment, Ben Bentley was 82-feet down inside the Wilkins well. Or if the Quilters Club was right, a well dug by Viking explorers.

Perhaps these Norsemen had spent a season here in Indiana, camping under this canopy of oak trees. That would have given them plenty of time to dig a well and carve messages on rocks that were later used by Benjamin Wilkins to build a protective wall around the well.

"How deep's the water?" Bombay Martinez

called down to him. Bombay was a retired circus performer. He worked with the Haney Bros. (actually a man and wife rather than brothers) at the zoo next to the Bentley farm. Among other duties, he took care of the elephant.

"Not very deep at all. Water only comes up to my knees." Ben was wearing his hip-waders that he used for duck hunting.

"Found any silver bars yet?"

"Nope. Nor any witch's bones. There *is* an aluminum Coke can floating down here, but I suspect it's of a more modern origin."

"Dastardly picnickers!" huffed Bombay. He hated litterbugs.

"Wait a minute, there's something here in the muck," called Ben's disembodied voice from deep in the well. "A glass jar with something in it. I'll put it in the bucket and you haul it up."

"Got it," replied Bombay, putting the winch in motion.

That was the only find of the day, the glass jar.

≈ ≈ ≈

After his frustrating meeting with that Historical Society lady, Maury Seiderman drove out to the Wilkins cottage. He could see people milling about in the distance, so he parked his

1975 LeSabre convertible on a side road and pulled out his Bausch and Lomb field glasses to spy on them. He wasn't sure what to do if these interlopers had found silver down there in the well.

Seiderman wasn't a violent man, but his partners were. His cousin's boyfriend had killed that Aitkens boy in some kind of argument over the stolen quilt. Maybe he'd call his cuz and let her boyfriend handle this if these people discovered the treasure.

But it didn't come to that. No silver bars were hauled up from the well. Just a Mason jar and that stocky guy in hip waders.

Chapter Sixteen

A Magic Potion

That evening the Quilters Club and their mates gathered around the butcher-block counter in Cookie Bentley's kitchen to study the artifact from the Wilkins well. It was a sealed Mason jar, the name showing in bas-relief on the glass side. Some kind of bloated shape could be seen floating in the murky brown liquid that filled the container.

"A Mason jar. That must be from a picnicker, like the Coke can," Lizzie sighed. Obviously disappointed with the singular find.

"Not necessarily," said Cookie. "Mason jars were patented on November 30, 1858 by John Landis Mason, a Philadelphia tinsmith. See, there's the date embossed on the side of the jar along with the name."

"This jar was made in 1858?" marveled Aggie,

standing on her tiptoes to see. She was still small for her age, practically the same height as her cousin N'yen.

"Probably not," Cookie shook her head. "Jars with that date on the side were manufactured well into the 1900s."

"But it has to be pretty old," said Ben. "Look how rusty that lid is."

"What's that blob inside?" asked N'yen. He squinted at the jar, the epicanthic folds making this eyes all the more narrow.

"Dunno," said his grandmother. "Maybe some old vegetable. A turnip or a cauliflower."

"Looks more like a chicken gizzard," Lizzie offered a guess. Not that she'd ever seen a chicken's gizzard in her life. She bought Tyson Farms roaster chickens, prepackaged and ready to slide into the oven. Cooking wasn't exactly her forte.

"I'd say it's a magic potion," guessed Cookie.

Beau Madison picked up the jar and shook it, just enough to stir up its contents. "Look, there's a lizard in there too."

"That looks like a tiny feather floating beside it."

Jim grimaced. "Hate to tell you, but that blob's

not a turnip or a gizzard. It's an eyeball. See, it just shifted so it's looking at you."

"*Eek*!" cried Aggie.

"I don't mean that it's really looking at you," he amended his words. "It just seems like it is."

"Can we open the jar?" asked N'yen.

"No," said the police chief. "I'm going to send it over to the state boys to let them analyze it. Better we don't break the seal."

"*Ooo*, a pickled eyeball," said Aggie. "Mad Matilda must've been a *really* wicked witch."

Chapter Seventeen

The Greater Midwest Occult Phenomena Association

Maury Seiderman hadn't been entirely honest with the town's mayor or the Historical Society lady. While it was true that he was a field investigator for G.M.O.P.A., he was also its president, its secretary, and its sergeant at arms. Matter of fact, he was the *only* member of the Greater Midwest Occult Phenomena Association.

Seiderman had grown up in Chicago, always a weird boy, perversely interested in the occult. The term comes from the Latin word *occultus*, meaning hidden or secret. For little Maury it included magic, mysticism, the paranormal, spiritualism, and theosophy. He subscribed to the Goodrick-Clarke thesis that occultism was "a strong desire to reconcile the findings of modern natural science with a religious view that could restore man to a position of centrality and dignity in the universe."

He was particularly fascinated by witchcraft and Satanism. The Feri Tradition founded by Victor Anderson and his wife Cora. Stregheria as popularized by Raven Grimassi. Raymond Bowers's Clan of the Tubal Cain. And especially the Order of the Trapezoid, led by Satan-worshiper Anton LaVey.

Perhaps this interest came from the fact he had a distant relative who'd claimed to be a witch – one Matilda Elizabeth Wilkins.

Seiderman had worked as a clerk at Borders, until the bookstore chain closed down. Now unemployed, he had nothing better to do than record stories of psychic phenomena he found online into the thick spiral-bound notebooks that lined the bookcases in his Irving Park apartment. This was the so-called database of G.M.O.P.A.

Even that was getting boring. So you can bet he was excited when his cousin called to ask if he'd help her and her boyfriend look for Viking silver that was described in runes embroidered on the Wilkins Witch Quilt. She knew he was good at research. All he had to do was follow the clues, like a scavenger hunt. She promised they would split the treasure equally, a third to each.

Seiderman had a plan. After he got his share of the treasure, he'd turn the other two in for the murder of that Aitkens boy. Maybe there was a reward. Or perhaps he could extract money from the boy's father. Everybody said Boyd Aitkens was richer than Croesus.

He'd have to go about it carefully. He didn't want to get arrested for extortion. Or as an accessory to murder. This called for a clever approach. But Maury's mother had always said he was a clever boy.

≈ ≈ ≈

Boyd Aitkens wasn't sure what to make of this odd-looking man who claimed to be an investigator for an Occult Phenomena Association. They were meeting in a back booth at the Cozy Café on South Main Street. The strange man obviously didn't want the two of them seen together.

"So what's this about?" demanded Aitkens. He was a large florid-faced farmer who had made a fortune growing watermelons. Normally, he didn't meet with nutcases, but this guy claimed he could tell Boyd who was responsible for his son's death.

"As you know, there are evil forces at large in this country," Maury Seiderman began his practiced spiel.

The farmer cut him off. "Look, Mr. Seiderman, I don't even go to church. So cut the crap about good and evil, and just tell me who killed my boy."

"It's not that simple."

"And why not?"

"Your land has been defiled. It was once the home of a witch." The man dug his fork into the slice of pie on the table before him. Cozy Café was known for its watermelon pie a la mode.

Boyd waved the words away. "Everybody knows about Mad Matilda. Around the turn of the century, she lived on a parcel of land that I now happen to own. She sold potions to gullible farmers. But what's that got to do with my son's murder?"

"Her bones lie at the bottom of that well next to the ruins of her cottage. So her spirit is not at rest. Her spirit entered a local man and enticed him to recover her quilt. Then it led this man to kill your son."

"Okay, I'll bite. Why?"

"Because your son disturbed her resting place by pumping water out of the well."

"If you say so. Now why did you ask for this meeting?"

"Because I can identify the man inhabited by Matilda Wilkins's spirit. The man who killed your son."

"You need to be talking to the police, not me."

The field investigator for G.M.O.P.A. finished off his pie, licked his lips, and said, "There are certain expenses involved in locating a wayward spirit. I hoped you might finance the exorcism."

"Finance? How much money are we talking here?"

"Forty thousand ought to do it."

Boyd Aitkens squinted his eyes, the muscles around his mouth tightening. "For forty G's you'll identify my son's murderer?"

"That is correct."

The watermelon farmer thought it over. "You bring me proof and the money's yours. But no proof, no payment."

Maury Seiderman frowned. "Might we discuss a small deposit?"

"No way, Jose." Boyd Aitkens stood up, towering over the occult investigator. "You don't get a thin dime till you identify the killer and I see proof of his guilt."

"You can count on it, sir." Maury stood up to shake the farmer's calloused hand. A deal struck. Now, after he located the silver, his cousin and her boyfriend were toast.

Chapter Eighteen

A Pickled Pig's Eye

"It was a pig's eye," Lt. Neil Wannamaker reported back to Chief Purdue. "Our forensic pathologist estimated it could be a hundred years old, pickled like that. Much of the tissue had deteriorated, but he had plenty for a DNA test. By the way, ISP will be invoicing your department for that test. Our budget's a little tight this year."

"Yours is tight? I don't even have one," carped Jim Purdue.

"So you think it was some kind of magical amulet?"

Jim sighed. "Something like that. Hard to say, but we're dealing with a self-professed witch."

"Any leads on that Aitkens boy's murder?"

"No," Jim lied. He had two very *good* leads from Harry the Hobbit. But he didn't feel like

139

sharing with the guy who had just stuck him with a $1,000 DNA testing bill. The Nail indeed.

≈ ≈ ≈

Harry Gertner had given them two names, fellow Tolkien fans who lived with single moms. Pinkus "Pinky" Bjork and Gary "the Gollum" Goldberg.

Deputy Pete Hitzer had promised to put Harry in a "witness protection program," meaning the police wouldn't reveal him as the source of these names.

The police chief's wife knew both boys. Bootsie sometimes worked as a substitute teacher when needed, so she recognized a lot of the local kids. She'd met Gary's parents, one of the few Jewish families in Caruthers Corners. Mariam Goldberg was separated from her husband Haim, but no one had filed for divorce yet. "Just a rough patch," she told her friends. Bootsie was pretty sure Mariam wasn't seeing anyone, trying hard to put her marriage back together.

That made Jim and his deputies focus on Pinky Bjork. Pinky was a withdrawn 16-year-old geek, spending most of his time online with various *Lord of the Rings* role-playing games, living a second-hand life as an avatar. His mother was a frazzled middle-aged blonde named Wanda. She'd been divorced from Bern Bjork, manager at the DQ, for about ten years now. Word had it that she was living with a guy who worked at the chair factory, an upholsterer named Ted Something-or-Other. Nobody knew much about him, but he quickly moved to the top of Chief Purdue's "Persons of Interest" list.

"Why do you want to talk with me and my son?" demanded Wanda Bjork when Deputy Hitzer showed up at her front door. The small brick-front bungalow was located on Jinks Lane, a narrow dead-end street named after one of the town's founders.

"We think your son might be able to help us with the missing quilt. Somebody said he's able to read those markings on the border of the quilt."

"Pinky's already translated those old markings," she smirked. "He's a very smart kid. Learned how to read that rune writing by playing his video games. Elves or dwarfs or one of them magical characters communicate with that language."

"Great. I'm sure he'll be a lot of assistance to us."

She eyed the deputy suspiciously. "Why do I

have to come along?" she asked, as if suspecting a trap.

"'Cause Pinky's underage. Gotta have a parent present when we interview him." True enough for the moment.

"Oh. That makes sense. Let me go get him. Can I ride up front, so the neighbors won't think I'm getting arrested?"

"No problem, ma'am. I'll wait here while you go fetch him." The deputy shifted his weight from foot to foot, a sign of impatience. But he displayed a polite smile, as fixed as the plastic face of a Halloween mask.

Three minutes later came a loud shriek.

Pete Hitzer dashed into the house and ran up the stairs. His 9mm Glock was in his hand. He encountered Wanda Bjorn standing in the narrow hallway, pointing into a bedroom.

"What?" he shouted.

"Pinky," she said. "He's gone."

≈ ≈ ≈

Chief Purdue personally picked up Ted Yost at the E-Z Chair factory. Wanda Bjorn confirmed that Yost was living with her, but denied any knowledge about the theft of the Wilkins Witch

Quilt. A search of her house turned up nothing.

She dutifully filled out a missing person report, but there would be no 24-hour waiting period in this case. Pinky was a material witness in a felony. The police chief already had two deputies scouring the town looking for him.

Ted Yost sat in the holding cell, whistling to himself like a man who didn't have a care in the world. He wore faded blue jeans and a red flannel shirt, the appearance of a working-class man. He said he didn't steal the quilt, but took the Fifth when asked who killed Charlie Aitkens.

Jim was pretty sure he'd solved the murder.

Lt. Neil Wannamaker phoned to say he was on the way to Caruthers Corners. *Yeah, come get involved now so you can take all the credit,* thought Jim in a flash of anger. But he didn't say anything.

When told of Ted Yost's arrest, Mayor Beau Madison figured this wrapped up the town's crime wave. It was pretty clear this guy Ted also stole the quilt. Edgar Ridenour had overheard it straight from the Aitkens boy. All that remained was to figure out where ol' Ted had stashed it.

As far as finding any Viking silver, Beau considered that to be a wild goose chase. There was no real proof Norsemen ever came to the Midwest. This "treasure" was a just a fantasy fostered by his wife and her Quilters Club buddies.

Boyd Aitkens phoned Beau to thank him for the support in finding his son's killer. The watermelon farmer assured him he could count on generous financial support come next election.

Heck, that wasn't such a big deal, thought Beau. He had only spent $2,000 in his last campaign. Twenty posters and a few radio ads.

Chapter Nineteen

Nothing Magic About Murder

Pinky Bjorn contacted his *Relic of the Runes* pal Harry the Hobbit. Little did he know Harry Gertner had given his name to the police in the first place.

As online gamers they used avatars, cyber characters that were fantastical improvements on their puny dateless real-life selves. Predictably, Pinky was an elf; Harry was a Hobbit. Both had magical powers, at least in the online world of *Relic of the Runes*.

"*Are the cops looking for me?*" Pinky typed into his laptop.

"*Cops? What for?*" replied the diminutive Hobbit on his screen.

"*I know who killed Charlie Aitkens.*"

"*Whoa, man. You better turn yourself in. That's serious stuff.*"

"No way. I'm responsible for the murder."

"How so?"

"I translated the runes on that witch quilt. If I hadn't done that, he wouldn't have stole it. And if he hadn't stole it he wouldn't have wound up killing Charlie over it."

"Who?"

"Can't say. But it's someone close to me."

"Your dad? Or Teddy Yost?"

"Can't say. Don't ask again or I will use fairy dust to immobilize you."

"Hobbits are immune to fairy dust."

"Says you."

≈ ≈ ≈

Meanwhile Ted Yost was refusing to talk. And Pinky Bjorn was still missing. Wanda Bjorn had been released for lack of evidence. Nothing tied her to either the missing quilt or the murder, not even Charlie Aitkens's own words.

With Charlie dead, the conversation overheard by Edgar Ridenour was being treated like a dying declaration. But Mark the Shark, now back from Milwaukee, told them it didn't meet the criteria for a deathbed confession, in that the boy's demise came days later.

Both Bill and Kathy had been released from

the Aurora St. Luke's Medical Center and were now back at home in Chicago. Little N'yen was torn between his anxiousness to see his mommy and daddy and an eagerness to help the Quilters Club solve this case. He wanted to see that Viking treasure with his very own eyes.

Aggie told him not to worry, that tomorrow's picnic was really just a cover story for their treasure hunt. With a little luck, he'd get to see the treasure before heading back to Chicago.

But that was before Spud Bodkin turned up.

≈ ≈ ≈

Spud had been on the run, fearful that the same fate would befall him as happened to his friend Charlie. He'd been holed up in an Indianapolis flea trap when Lt. Wannamaker tracked him down. Spud had used his credit card to pay for the room, a mistake when the police are looking for you.

"Honest, I was gonna turn myself in," he lied to the state policeman.

"Sure you were," said Wannamaker.

"I didn't even know you wanted to talk with me till yesterday. Saw my picture on TV."

"Well, here you are – so talk."

"I didn't kill Charlie."

Wannamaker leaned back in his chair, one of two in the bare ISP Interrogation Room. Folding chairs, metal table, one-way glass on the wall – the room's total furnishings. "Didn't think you did," said the lieutenant.

Spud wrinkled his forehead. With his round face, thick glasses, and protruding ears, he did look a bit like Mr. Potato Head. "Then why were you looking for me?"

"Thought you could tell me who stole the Wilkins Witch Quilt. Valued at over a hundred grand, that makes it a felony."

"Wasn't me."

"But you know who did. Someone overheard you and Charlie Aitkens talking."

"Was that who killed Charlie, the eavesdropper?"

Wannamaker shook his head slowly, like the pendulum of a ticking clock. "Nope. We think it was the fellow who stole the quilt, trying to shut you guys up."

"That was my thought too. That's why I took off when I heard Charlie was dead."

"How'd you hear?"

"On the radio."

"So who is this fellow you're afraid of, the one

who stole the quilt. We'll pick him up and then you'll be as safe as a babe in his mother's arms."

"Sure. I don't mind telling you – our ol' pal Bern."

"Who the fudge is that?"

≈ ≈ ≈

Chief Purdue was confused by the phone call he got from Neil the Nail. "What do you mean you've identified the quilt thief as Bern Bjorn? I've got the guilty party locked up right here in my holding cell, a guy named Theodore Yost. Works at the local chair factory."

"No," insisted the ISP lieutenant. "It's a fellow named Bern Bjork. Go pick him up. Me and my boys will be there in about two hours if the traffic's light."

"Can't be Bern Bjorn," insisted Jim Purdue. "Bern manages the local Dairy Queen. He gives me extra sprinkles every time I go in."

"You better have him in custody by the time we get there or I'll give you enough sprinkles to choke on."

"Hey, watch your tone. You said the murder was my case to solve. And I have – Ted Yost."

"Well, the art theft is *my* case and I just solved it – Bern Bjorn."

"But the same guy that stole the quilt killed Charlie Aitkens."

"Exactly," said the Nail, hanging up in the police chief's ear.

Chapter Twenty

Searching for the Viking Treasure

With two separate suspects under arrest, the Quilters Club turned its attention back to the Viking treasure. Cookie was convinced it was buried at the site of the Church of Avenging Angels. Where else could it be, now that the well had proved to be a "dry hole."

"Dry?" laughed her husband Ben. "There was a good three feet of water in that old well. Came up to my hoo-ha."

"Your what?"

"Never mind. Let me just say my waders had a leak and that water was icy cold. Thought I'd freeze my –"

"Ben!"

"Like I said, never mind."

She smiled. They had married late in life. While she'd been a widow, he'd been an old bachelor. As such, Ben Bentley still got tongue-tied around his wife when risqué subjects came up.

"Point is, you found nothing down in that well. Not even the bones of Mad Matilda.

"There was that Mason jar," he reminded her.

She rolled her eyes. "A magic amulet of some kind. But nothing to do with a Viking treasure."

"True."

"So if the silver's not there in the well, the men who killed Matilda Wilkins must have taken it."

Ben was eating a bowl of cereal, his mouth full. "Tha iz gun."

"What's that you said?"

He swallowed, then repeated: "Then it's gone. You'll never find it if the old woman's killers took it. The law never found them."

"There's an old legend that says they buried the money under the steps of their church. All we have to it find where it stood and look there."

"What church was that?" Ben knew the countryside around Caruthers Corners like the back of his hand. Having worked one summer as a surveyor of watermelon-growing allotments, he'd traveled every square inch of the county.

"The Church of Avenging Angels."

"Never heard of it." Ben refilled his bowl with

puffed rice. He was fond of that snap-crackle-pop cereal.

"The church burned down in 1899. Nobody remembers where it stood."

"Like I said, the treasure's long gone."

"No, we just have to figure out where the church used to be."

"Ga tal t' Heni Guna."

"Don't talk with your mouth full, dear."

He swallowed. "Go talk to Howard Gunnar. He's the oldest man in town. Maybe he'll know."

≈ ≈ ≈

N'yen and his cousin Agnes were watching television, a movie called *The Black Pirate* starring Douglas Somebody as a guy who pretends to be a pirate in order to rescue a princess. "Aw, they stole that plot from *The Princess Bride*. They just changed the name from 'the Dread Pirate Roberts' to 'the Black Pirate.'"

"I think *The Black Pirate* came first," said Aggie.

"When those pirates said, 'Dead men tell no tales,' it reminded me of the murder we're trying to solve."

"How so?" asked his cousin. Their grandmother had made them popcorn with lots of butter. AMC was running a day of buccaneer movies.

"Because the guy that stole the quilt killed that Charlie guy to keep him from telling tales."

"You're pretty smart for a boy," she complimented him.

"Thanks. Now all we gotta do is figure out which one is guilty, the man who works at the chair factory or the one who manages the Dairy Queen."

"Maybe they're both guilty."

"Naw, I think it's the frozen custard guy."

"Why's that?"

"That boy who translated the secret message would have told his dad. I know I would've."

"You're pretty fond of your dad, huh?"

"Don't remember my real dad. But Bill is about the best-est dad ever. I'd tell him anything. Sure hope he's okay."

"Don't worry. My daddy's up there making sure he's okay. Your mom too."

"Dads and moms are great, aren't they? I didn't have any for the longest time. Now I've got a whole family, including you."

"I like my grandmother a lot," admitted Aggie.

"And I like my grampy," N'yen added. "He

doesn't care that I'm adoptated."

"Adopted, you mean."

"Yeah, that. It's kinda special when you think about it. Out of all the boys and girls in the world, Bill and Kathy picked me."

≈ ≈ ≈

It took Cookie all morning to round up the Quilters Club. Lizzie was already at the Garden Club Luncheon. Bootsie was baking a watermelon cake for Jim. And Maddy was working on her latest patchwork quilt while the kids watched movies on AMC.

In addition, Cookie had to contact Howard Gunnar's great-granddaughter to arrange for a visit. The old man tired easily, she was told, but would receive them following his afternoon nap.

"Howard Gunnar, that's a good idea," said Maddy. "If anyone remembers the location of that church, it would be him."

"Ben suggested it."

"You've got yourself a good man, Cookie. Going down in that well for you. Giving that land to Haney Bros. Circus to establish a town zoo. Supporting our misadventures."

"Don't I know it! He's my very own teddy bear." Although Ben Bentley had had a crush on Cookie since high school, it was only after her first husband died in a tractor accident that they got together.

"We're all lucky gals," said Maddy. "Finding good men to share our lives with."

"And we're lucky to have each other as friends," Cookie replied – meaning the Quilters Club.

≈ ≈ ≈

Howard Gunnar had celebrated his 100th birthday only last month. Mayor Beauregard Madison had declared the day as "The Howard Gunnar Centennial" and presented the old man with a bronze plaque to that effect. The *Burpyville Gazette* ran his picture on the front page. His great-granddaughter Roberta had accompanied Howard to the ceremony on the town square.

The Quilters Club arrived in mass at the Gunnar farm. Surrounded by the expanding town limits, the ten-acre farm was abutted on three sides by residential streets and new housing. No crops had been grown there in forty years, other than a few assorted vegetables in the small garden plot behind the weathered farmhouse.

"They're expecting us, right?" asked Maddy Madison. She believed in good manners.

Cookie nodded vigorously. "Yes, I spoke to

Roberta Gunnar. She's Howard's caretaker as well as his only living relative."

"I brought watermelon cake," said Bootsie. "Jim told me the old man is fond of it."

"I wouldn't mind a slice myself," grumbled Lizzie. "I didn't have any lunch."

"Me either," Bootsie admitted, eyeing the cake platter in her hands.

"Behave yourself, you're on a diet," Maddy reminded her friend.

"I'm not," said Lizzie. Still as slender as when she was as a high-school cheerleader.

"What do you mean you didn't have lunch?" accused Cookie. "You were at the Garden Club bash."

"Nobody ever eats at those things. Rubber chicken and talk-talk-talk."

"Come along, girls," urged Maddy. "Maybe Mr. Gunnar will share a slice or two with you."

"He better," muttered Bootsie. "I actually baked it for Jim."

"We appreciate his sacrifice," said Maddy as she stepped onto the farmhouse porch.

Roberta Gunnar was a thirtysomething brunette with plump hips and generous thunder thighs. However, she had a radiant smile, all the more noticeable with her whitened teeth. "Come inside," she invited, holding the door wide. "Gramps is in the living room."

"We brought him cake," Bootsie announced, hold it up for all to see.

"Watermelon cake? That's his favorite."

"So we heard."

The old man looked something like a mummy, given his wrinkled gray skin and wispy hair. But his watery brown eyes twinkled with alertness. "Don't get many visitors anymore," he nodded his welcome. "Everybody I know is long dead – friends, children, even grandchildren. Nobody left but Roberta here. Guess I'll be joining them friends and relatives soon enough."

"Aw Gramps, you're gonna live forever," his great-granddaughter said.

"Sure looks like it, don't it. Never expected to see a hundred. They gave me a nice party last month."

Cookie broached the subject. "We wanted to ask you about an old landmark."

"Landmark? I've never traveled farther than Indianapolis."

"A local landmark. A church that's long gone," explained Maddy.

"Church, you say? Never was much of a churchgoer. Course I may regret that soon enough."

"We're trying to find out where the Church of Avenging Angels was located," said Bootsie, handing him a slice of watermelon cake. A bribe as it were.

"Avenging Angels? That was even before my time. I'm only a hundred years old. That church burned down 'fore I was born."

"But did anyone ever show you where it was located?" asked Lizzie, eying his cake with envy.

"Ever show me? No. But my daddy told me it was on the other side of Never Ending Swamp, over near Gruesome Gorge."

"Can you be more specific?" pleaded Cookie.

"Not really. My daddy didn't think much of them Avenging Angels. Said they was witch hunters from St. Paul. Told me they killed a local woman for being a witch."

"You mean Matilda Wilkins?" Bootsie coached.

"That's her, Mad Matilda. My daddy said she flew about on a broomstick. Changed people into frogs. Put curses on her enemies. Guess it didn't work with them Avenging Angels. They threw her down her own well."

"But their church −?"

"Told you, never seen it. Was burnt down 'fore I was born. I told you that, didn't I?"

"Gramps forgets what he says," Roberta explained in a stage whisper.

"I can hear you, girl," he admonished his great-granddaughter. "Lost my smell. But I still got my hearing."

"You say it was burnt?" Cookie pressed.

"To the ground. The posse that was looking for them did it, my daddy said. They was snake handlers. My daddy said rattlers came crawling outta the fire like creatures from hell."

"Snakes!" squeaked Lizzie. She had an aversion to snakes, mice, spiders, and bees.

"Rattlers fat as my forearm," the old man said. Enjoying having shocked his audience. "The preacher that led the Avenging Angels used to sleep with diamondbacks, according to my daddy. Said them snakes never bit him, like they were akin."

"Rev. Billingsley Royce, you mean?" prodded Cookie.

"Don't recall his name. Daddy said he had the mark of Cain on him."

"About the church −?"

"This sure is tasty cake," muttered the old man. "Can I have another slice?"

"Yes, of course. Now about the church –?"

"Pretty day, ain't it?"

≈ ≈ ≈

Another dead end. Cookie Bentley was pretty despondent. Excusing herself, saying she had work to do, she went back to her office. The Historical Society had recently moved into a small building on North Main Street. The town council thought it could become a tourist attraction, so the front room served as a museum with a permanent exhibit about the history of Caruthers Corners.

• A copy of Indiana's proclamation of statehood.

• A six-foot-tall wooden Indian in native costume.

• A first-rate collection of arrowheads and pottery.

• Bronze busts of the town's founders – Jacob Caruthers, Ferdinand Jinks, and Col. Beauregard Madison.

• A diorama of the Big Fire of 1899.

• Architectural drawings of the Town Hall.

• A 3-D model of the E-Z Chair factory.

- A video showing highlights from the annual Watermelon Days festival.
- A horticultural poster on growing watermelons.
- A display of prizewinning patchwork quilts.
- That rare copy of *A Personal History of Caruthers Corners and Surrounding Environs* by Martin Caruthers.
- Photos of local buildings.
- An antique bottle collection.
- A circus poster showing the Haney Bros. on each side of Happy the Elephant.
- Edwin the Enchanted Doll, basis of a local ghost story.
- A collection of carnival glass.
- An aerial photograph of Caruthers Corners.

The backroom was officially designated as the secretary's office, but it was more of a storeroom with a wooden desk in the center. File cabinets and stacks of newspapers lined the walls. Boxes of uncatalogued artifacts took one corner. Shelves of donated antiques occupied another corner. An ancient cuckoo ticked over the doorway.

Cookie was putting away the newspaper clippings about the death of Matilda Wilkins when she spotted the albumin photograph of Rev. Billingsley Royce. She paused to study the faded image. His slightly crossed eyes had a crazed look. That wine-stain could certainly be interpreted as a mark of Cain. He was frowning, a sign of his disapproval of the ungodly world around him.

Idly turning the photograph over, she discovered an inked notation on its backside: *Taken on the 12 August 1897 at the church at Steppin Rock.*

Hmm, where had she heard that name before? Wasn't Steppin' Rock an oddly shaped limestone formation out near Gruesome Gorge? Could that have been the location of the Church of Avenging Angels?

This called for another field trip for the Quilters Club. But they would have to call it a "picnic" for the benefit of their unsympathetic spouses. The boys considered the case closed. But Cookie knew better.

Chapter Twenty-One

Steppin' Rock

Nobody seemed to recall where Steppin' Rock was located. Wasn't like it was a big tourist attraction. Just a colorful name given to a natural rock formation that didn't even appear on area maps.

Maddy used the picnic excuse to ask her husband. Beau didn't have a clue about it, though he'd lived all his life in Caruthers Corners. So had she. In fact, so had all the members of the Quilters Club and their husbands.

At Maddy's prodding, Beau checked with the Planning and Zoning Department, Public Works, and the Tax Assessor's Office ... but none of them knew where to find Steppin' Rock.

The Quilters Club may as well have been asking how to find the Church of Avenging Angels. Or maybe they were, in so many words.

Despite Ben Bentley's watermelon-allotment surveying, Edgar Ridenour's fishing excursions, or Chief Jim Purdue's patrols, no one had ever been to Steppin' Rock. Yet they all had heard the name, a local rock formation.

Young N'yen came through with the solution. He'd seen a movie where Osama ben Laden's hideout had been observed from satellite photos. *Zero Dark Thirty*, it was called. Maddy was aghast that the child had been allowed to see such a violent film. But Bill and Kathy were very liberal in their childrearing, as with most things.

"Satellite photos," laughed Lizzie. "Where would we get those?"

Maddy had the answer. "Not satellite images, but aerial plat maps for the entire county are stored in the Town Hall's basement."

"How would we ever find Steppin' Rock among all those rolls of aerial photographs. There must be a zillion of them down there," frowned Bootsie.

Cookie solved that one. "We don't have to look at all of them. Just the photos around Gruesome Gorge on the far side of Never Ending Swamp. That's where Howard Gunnar said it was located."

"That narrows it down some," Bootsie acquiesced.

≈ ≈ ≈

After two dusty hours in the Town Hall basement, they found it, Aerial Photo R-790-3. There it was – a rectangular rock slab. Even so, they would have likely missed it if someone hadn't written STEPPINGSTONE ROCK next to it with a red grease pencil.

"Steppingstone?" said Lizzie doubtfully. "That's not right."

Maddy squinted at the oversized photo. "That's got to be it."

"Um, I dunno."

"Well –"

"One way to find out," suggested precocious Aggie. "Let's go look."

Chapter Twenty-Two

Digging for the Viking Silver

The outcropping known locally as Steppin' Rock was located just inside the boundaries of Gruesome Gorge State Park. It was a flat sandstone boulder that looked like the foundation of a house. Supposedly, the rock had been the site of a Potawatomi sweat lodge.

A Personal History of Caruthers Corners and Surrounding Environs told how the Potawatomi had been members of the Council of Three Fires, along with the Ojibwe and the Ottawa. Although their tribal name translated as "keepers of the fire," they were considered younger brothers of the Council.

The leader of these Wabash Potawatomi was known as Winamac (meaning "Catfish"). He and his Fish Clan had sided with the British during the war of 1812. They were the ones who had attacked the wagon train led by Col. Beauregard Madison, Jacob Caruthers, and Ferdinand Jinks – the battle that led to the founding of Caruthers Corners.

Actually, there had been two Chief Winamacs, one an opponent of the US, the other an ally. The "bad" Winamac had made his camp at Gruesome Gorge.

Maddy Madison walked across the sandstone surface of Steppin' Rock, Aggie and N'yen following two steps behind. "So the Indians built a sweat lodge atop this outcropping?" she mused aloud.

"What's a sweat lodge?" asked Aggie.

"Kind of like a sauna."

"You mean this was an Indian health spa?"

"Not exactly." Maddy didn't want to tell her granddaughter how this settlement near Gruesome Gorge had proven quite unhealthy for the Native Americans who had died here in an ambush.

"Martin J. Caruthers wrote about the Potawatomi sweat lodge in his history book," Cookie noted. "But he didn't mention Steppin' Rock." She was standing on the sidelines, watching as Bootsie and Liz measured the boulder's squarish surface with a tape measure. Members of the Quilters Club always carried tape measures for checking out fabrics and quilting squares.

"Eighteen by twenty feet," Bootsie called out. "Plenty big for a sweat lodge."

"Eighteen and a half," Lizzie corrected.

"Eighteen and a half," Bootsie repeated to acknowledge the adjusted figure.

Maddy ran her hand across the reddish-brown surface, as smooth as if it had been planed and leveled. "This makes a natural foundation," she noted. "A perfect place to build a sweat lodge."

"What if Rev. Billingsley Royce and his followers built their church here too? Any remnants of a sweat lodge would have been long gone by the 1890s," Cookie posed the question. "After all, it *said* Steppin' Rock on the back of that photograph."

Maddy's gaze swept the outcropping. "If this were the site of a country church, where would the front door have been?"

"Over here, most likely," pointed Cookie. "The ground slopes. That makes the far side too high off the ground, I'd guess."

"Didn't the story say they buried the treasure

under the church steps?" asked Lizzie, always an eye on the money.

"The steps would've been right here," said Bootsie, "if Cookie's right about the door." The ground looked undisturbed, the rock's shadow forming a triangle on the grass.

"That looks about right," nodded Maddy.

"Should we dig?" Bootsie asked. She sounded uneasy.

"Why wouldn't we?"

"Well, this *is* state park land."

"We're on a picnic," reasoned Maddy. "Wouldn't it be proper camping etiquette to dig a fire pit for our weenie roast? You know, to prevent forest fires and such."

"Oh boy," exclaimed little N'yen. "We're gonna have hot dogs!"

≈ ≈ ≈

Two hours later there was a pile of dirt the size of a Volkswagen next to the hole they'd dug, but no silver bars had been found.

"Guess we got this one wrong," sighed Cookie. In her enthusiasm, she'd done much of the digging. Tomorrow her back would be the devil to pay.

"Not necessarily," said Maddy. She'd been reassessing the situation. "Maybe the story got garbled. Instead of the treasure being buried under the church's steps, maybe it was buried under Steppin' Rock."

Bootsie laughed. "You mean under this giant slab of sandstone? No way."

"Maybe not under the entire rock, but under a corner of it," suggested Maddy. She studied the reddish-brown sandstone platform, looking for a likely entry point.

"We've dug four feet down and haven't come to the bottom of the rock," Cookie groused.

Bootsie rubbed her back. "Will Rogers said, 'If you find yourself in a hole, stop digging.'"

"Thanks for the helpful advice." Lizzie's tone meant just the opposite.

Maddy hadn't given up. "Perhaps we can get under it better on the other side. With the ground sloping, there's already four or five feet of rock showing over there."

Cookie acquiesced. "One small hole just to see how deep this rock goes."

Ten minutes later, Cookie said, "There it is, the bottom of this big slab of sandstone."

Steppin' Rock proved to be about six-feet thick. The remnant of a long-ago ice age, when glaciers moved boulders about like a game of marbles.

"Now dig under the edge," instructed Maddy.

"Hey, your turn."

"Oh, all right," said Maddy, stepping into the hole and taking the shovel.

Another ten minutes. "Anything yet?" asked Lizzie, trying to peer into the hole. Maddy had been tunneling under the bottom of the rock.

"Nothing. And my back's getting tired. Want to take over Lizzie?"

Lizzie grimaced. "No more digging for me. I've already broken a fingernail."

"Here, I'll dig for a while," volunteered Bootsie.

Ten minutes more. "The shovel just struck something solid," announced Bootsie. Sounding excited.

"Is it a silver bar?" Lizzie asked.

"Not sure."

"Brush away the dirt," ordered Maddy, taking charge as usual. "Let's see what you've found."

Bootsie bent down to scoop the dirt away with her hands. A rounded shape came into view. "Oh, shoot," she said. "Just another rock."

"Pull it out and keep digging," said Cookie. "Maybe there's something behind it."

"Your turn. I'm tired."

Cookie Bentley took the shovel. She'd borrowed it from her husband's toolshed this morning before setting out on this "picnic." Scraping away the loose dirt, the rock became more defined. An oblong chunk of limestone, about the size of a loaf of bread. "If there's another stone behind this one, I'm quitting. This was a stupid idea."

"Wasn't it your idea?" Lizzie asked with a false innocence.

"Rub it in," sighed Cookie. "I deserve it."

"Here," said Maddy, climbing into the hole with Cookie. "Let me help you pull it out."

The two women struggled with the rock, wiggling it side to side. It was starting to give. "On the count of three," said Maddy. "One ... two ... THREE!"

With a *pop!* the rock slid out, leaving a dark hole. "Okay," said Cookie, "unless there's a Viking sword and a bar of silver in there, I'm going home."

"Hey," wailed N'yen. "What about the hot

dogs?"

≈ ≈ ≈

Maury Seiderman was lurking behind a large oak tree, a good vantage point for spying on those busybody women from Caruthers Corners. He recognized the one from the Historical Society. What were they doing out here?

He'd been scouting the area in his '75 LeSabre, looking for ruins of a church. Nothing. Just watermelon fields and grassy countryside. An occasional Amish farmhouse, identifiable by the lack of power lines. Then he'd spotted the SUV filled with women and kids. That Bentley woman from the Historic Society had been sitting there in the front seat, big as life. So he'd decided to follow them. They had led him down an unmarked cow path along the upper rim of Gruesome Gorge. Could they be looking for the treasure too?

Now he knew the answer.

They were pulling something out from under that big sandstone outcropping. Obviously, they had found the Viking silver.

Chapter Twenty-Three

Down to No Suspects

Chief Purdue didn't like it one bit, but he had to cut Ted Yost free. No evidence, other than he was dating the mother of a *Lord of the Rings* fanboy. No crime in that, Lt. Wannamaker pointed out.

The police chief had brought in Bern Bjorn, just as Neil the Nail had instructed. That meant no more free sprinkles for him. Bern was pretty irked.

In the end, he'd had to let Bern Bjorn go too. Came down to the word of Lt. Wannamaker's witness versus Bern's. No real evidence.

Quite a coincidence that Bern was the ex-husband of Ted's girlfriend. But this was a small town, a population of 2,577 give or take.

"Back to square one," grumbled Wannamaker, as if it were Jim's fault he'd taken the word of an unemployed ne'er-do-well over that of a local business owner.

"Yeah, I'll be in touch if I turn up anything new," said the police chief, his sarcasm as thick as watermelon jam.

"You do that."

"I'm not paying that invoice for the DNA testing. It was a clue."

"It was a hundred-year-old pig's eye, for goodness sake."

"We didn't know that till we tested it."

"You wasted the time of the state lab."

"That's what it's there for, to help us examine clues."

"Magic potions aren't clues."

"D'you think we'll ever find the Wilkins Witch Quilt?"

"Naw," admitted Wannamaker. "I've got a feeling that quilt's gone for good. Probably already in the hands of some private collector where it will never again see the light of day."

≈ ≈ ≈

Pinky Bjorn was hiding in Burpyville at the home of his cousin. He hadn't phoned his mother, afraid she'd tell the police where to find him.

Somehow they had connected him with stealing that old quilt. Not that he'd had any active part in the burglary. But he knew who did. After all, he was the one who had translated those runes. Pretty simple when you'd spent the last two years playing *Relic of the Runes*, an online Tolkien-inspired game that required a basic knowledge of Scandinavian *Futhark* or its Anglo-Saxon variant called *Futhorc*.

The *Early Futhorc* was identical to the *Elder Futhark*, except for the split the a-rune into three variants, resulting in 26 runes. No harder to learn than the ABC alphabet, truth be known.

He'd been there in the Town Hall waiting for his mother to pay her property tax when he noticed that quilt hanging on the wall. He remembered being fascinated by its depiction of angels and devils fighting each other. Cool beans. Like a video game. Then he noticed the symbols around the quilt's border, clearly runes.

It took him less than fifteen minutes to decipher them. He was working from memory, without any reference books. But after two years of playing *Relic of the Runes* he was getting pretty good at it. He held the rank of Exalted Grand Wizard of the Elfin World.

The message went something like "After a long journey, we are hiding our money in deep water." He didn't know why anybody would put that on an old quilt, but it sounded like a clue on a treasure map. Money hidden in deep water ... you'd have to know something about the old woman who made the quilt to figure that out.

The bronze plaque on the wall said this Matilda Wilkins claimed to be a witch. She must have been nuts. He didn't believe in witches, although he *did* believe in wizards, elves, and Hobbits. He wondered if the old woman had lived around here? And did she have a pond or a well?

He'd have to ask somebody about that, he remembered thinking. Now he was sorry he'd ever seen that blasted quilt. Or told anybody about the message. How did he know that the person he'd confided in would steal it!

≈ ≈ ≈

Ted Yost went straight home, where Wanda was waiting for him. "Have you heard from Pinky?" he asked the boy's mother.

"Not a word."

"The police are still looking for him."

Wanda pressed her fingertips against her temples, as if suffering from a severe migraine.

"W-what did you tell them?"

"Nothing. I clammed up, took the Fifth."

"Thank you for protecting Pinky."

"Your boy didn't have anything to do with stealing the quilt. We both know that."

"But he translated those symbols on the Wilkins Witch Quilt. They might arrest him as an accomplice."

"Nobody knows he broke the quilt's code. We've just gotta keep our mouths shut and he'll be all right. They can't prove anything."

"How do you know that?"

"Why else would they have let *me* go?"

Chapter Twenty-Four

Another Pig's Eye

"This is not a silver bar," said Maddy, holding up a dirt-encrusted Mason jar.

Cookie asked, "What's in it? Another pig's eye."

"I can't tell." She rubbed at the dirt off the glass. "There's something inside. Pebbles or something."

"Open it," urged Lizzie. Her red hair blazing in the noonday sun.

"No way," barked Bootsie, taking the shovel from Maddy. "It might be evidence that only the police should handle."

"Can't open it anyway," said Maddy, having tried. "The lid's rusted shut."

"I'll open it," said a strange voice. Everyone looked up to see an odd-looking man standing above them on the sandstone slab. He was as slender as Jack Skellington. A thin mustache crossed his upper lip. His raven-black hair was slicked back with a thick gel. In his hand he held an ugly-looking P-08 parabellum Luger. "Give that jar to me," he ordered, "or I'll shoot."

"Hey, who's that man?" asked little N'yen, confused by the intruder's sudden appearance.

"That's Maury Seiderman," answered Cookie Bentley. "He's with some paranormal research organization." She couldn't quite remember the name on his business card.

"The Greater Midwest Occult Phenomena Association," he reminded her haughtily. "By now you've probably figured out I'm on the same mission as you: To find the Viking silver that Rev. Billingsley Royce took from Matilda Wilkins."

"Well, it's certainly not in this jar," said Maddy, handing it up to him. "Last Mason jar we found contained spunk water, feathers, and a pig's eye."

"A witch's potion," he snorted.

"Exactly. This is probably something similar."

"Open it."

"Can't. It's rusted shut."

"Lemme take a look at it," he ordered. Tucking the pistol under his belt, he attempted to twist the lid but it refused to open. "*Umph!*" he grunted, face twisted with the exertion.

"Told you," said Maddy.

"Oh well," shrugged Maury Seiderman, then smashed the Mason jar against the unyielding surface of Steppin' Rock.

Kra-ack!

"You shouldn't've done that," admonished Aggie. "The jar didn't belong to you, Mr. Seiderman. We found it, so it was ours – fair and square."

"Too bad, so sad, little missy," he sneered. "Mine now because I've got the gun."

"Not for long," said Bootsie as she swung the shovel – *klang!* – knocking the Luger from his hand.

"Ow," he cried, stepping back.

Lizzie retrieved the gun, but in her hands it looked about as effective as a child holding a bazooka. She didn't even have her finger on the trigger. Probably afraid of smudging her nail polish, Cookie joked later. "Stop right there, buster!" barked Lizzie with enough authority to stop Maury Seiderman in his tracks.

"Look, ladies, this was just a joke," he pleaded. "I saw you digging down here and thought I might have some fun."

"With a gun?" retorted Bootsie. She often accompanied her husband to the shooting range out on Field Hand Road so she knew the damage a bullet could do. Sometimes they used watermelons as targets, making a big red splash when the 9mm slug hit its target.

"That pistol's not even loaded," he said.

"Then it will be okay if I point it at your head and pull the trigger," smiled Lizzie. She adjusted her aim, one eye squinted.

"No, wait. Don't do that. Gun safety and all."

"Right," said Lizzie, shifting her finger to pull the trigger.

Ka-bam!

The bullet zinged past Maury Seiderman's ear. "Holy rollers, you almost killed me," he shouted at her.

"I thought you said it wasn't loaded."

"Good thing you're a lousy shot," he muttered, a tremor in his voice.

"Right," said Lizzie. Not volunteering that she and Edgar often went to the shooting range with Jim and Bootsie. She was actually a very good shot.

Maddy spoke up: "Perhaps you don't mind

telling us what you're doing out here waiving a gun around?"

"Looking for the treasure," he muttered. "I've got as much right to it as you have. Maybe more. I'm related to Matilda Wilkins on my mother's side. She was a Süderdithmarschen – although the family shortened it to Marsch generations ago."

"So you're not really an occult researcher?"

"Of course I am. That's why my cousin called me in to help locate the family treasure."

Bootsie had been talking on her cell phone. "Jim has a deputy on the way," she announced as she hung up.

"The police?" Seiderman offered a weak smile. "C'mon, we don't need to get them involved, do we?"

"When you start waving guns at the police chief's wife, the police get involved," stated Bootsie, an angry set to her jaw.

"Hey now –"

"Don't try to run away," warned Maddy. "Our friend Lizzie could have shot your ear off, if she'd wanted too."

"Okay, okay. But this is all a silly misunderstanding."

"I've got a question," said little Aggie.

Hanging back, with a protective arm around her younger cousin.

"Yes dear?" Maddy turned to her granddaughter.

"What was in the jar he broke?"

Chapter Twenty-Five

The Shattered Mason Jar

Everybody circled the shattered Mason jar there on the sandstone surface of Steppin' Rock. The syrupy water formed a puddle, like a miniature pond with a couple of feathers and another eyeball floating in it.

"Aw shucks, another jar of goo," said Lizzie.

"A witch's potion," Cookie corrected her.

"Is that an eyeball?" squealed Aggie, pointing at the greasy orb. Yellowish from a century of slow pickling.

"Yes, dear," said Cookie, patting the girl's shoulder. "Probably another pig's eye."

"No silver?" grumbled their prisoner.

"Not an ounce," said Lizzie, sounding equally disappointed.

"Nothing to do but wait," sighed Bootsie, putting her cell phone back in her purse. "Deputy

Hitzer will be here in another ten minutes."

≈ ≈ ≈

Beau Madison was sitting at his desk. Being mayor was quite an honor, but sometimes he didn't feel up to the task. Life had been much simpler when he ran the small Ace Hardware on South Main Street. Had he accepted the mayoral position out of fear of competing with the big Home Depot outside of town? Yes, probably.

Maybe he should just retire, take his Social Security, draw on his 401k, and spend more time with his grandkids. Little N'yen was fast becoming his favorite.

Let someone else worry about stolen quilts, witches, and Viking treasure ...

Chapter Twenty-Six

The Witch's Great-Great Granddaughter

That next day at 9 a.m. Cookie Bentley met her Quilters Club pals for coffee at the Cozy Diner. You could tell she was excited by the way she nervously batted her eyes, the lashes fluttering like twin butterflies. "Last night I was doing some more research," she gushed. "And I may have stumbled onto something important to the case."

"I thought the case was pretty much over," replied Maddy Madison. "The police have given up on finding the missing quilt. Charlie Aitkens's murderer may never be solved. Maury Seiderman is in jail for threatening us with a pistol. And as we've discovered, there's no Viking treasure."

"Maybe there's no treasure," said Cookie. "But

I think the Quilters Club can still solve the theft and murder.”

“Do tell,” said Bootsie. A little defensive of her husband Jim’s failed efforts.

Cookie mistakenly took that as a go-ahead. “I decided to do a little more digging on Matilda Elizabeth Wilkins to see if she has any living relatives.”

“And –?”

“I found one,” said the town’s historian.

Maddy said, “You mean, Maury Seiderman?”

“No, someone else – his cousin.”

“You’re saying you were able to piece together the old woman’s genealogy chart?” asked Lizzie, always impressed with lineage.

“Well, not me. I went online to YourAncestors.com and looked up Matilda Wilkins. The website taps into everything from birth records to wedding licenses.”

Maddy sipped at her coffee. No chicory to her disappointment. “Surely they didn’t have any of that stuff back in the mid 1800s when Mad Matilda was born...”

“Lots of people share Family Bible listings as well as their own genealogical research with the website. Happens, one of Matilda Wilkins’s relatives had filled in the genealogy chart pretty well. And recently too."

"Who?" said Lizzie.

"Yes, who?" repeated Bootsie.

"Do we know this relative?" echoed Maddy.

Cookie paused to build up the suspense. "As a matter of fact, you do. The clue was in that history book by Martin Caruthers. He referred to her as Mrs. Wilkins. Matilda married one Benjamin Wilkins back in 1892. He died shortly after that. Her maiden name on the marriage certificate was Süderdithmarschen. That's a Germanic or Old Norse name."

"Maury Seiderman told us that yesterday," said Lizzie. "That's nothing new."

"Yes, but he said the name got shortened to Marsch. Remember?"

"Oh my," gasped Maddy. "Beau's new secretary is Becky Marsch."

"Bingo," said Cookie. "It was none other than Rebecca Matilda Marsch who posted the updated genealogical chart on YourAncestor.com. She's Mad Matilda's great-great granddaughter on the old witch's brother's side of the family. Maury Seiderman's first cousin."

"Are you suggesting Becky stole the quilt?"

asked Bootsie, always looking for a culprit. A policeman's wife through and through.

"In a sense. I think she provided the Town Hall's alarm code to the actual thief. We always knew it was an inside job, but everybody kept focusing on that ol' reprobate, Jasper Beanie. He was just a red herring."

"Becky Marsch," Maddy repeated the name as if trying to get used to this new theory. Her husband's secretary of all people!

"Why did she do it?" asked Lizzie.

"The money?" said Bootsie. "The thrill? Because she didn't get a big enough raise?"

"Maybe Becky wanted to reclaim something she thought rightfully belonged to her family," speculated Maddy.

"I suppose I could understand that," said Bootsie. "But she certainly went about it the wrong way."

"Don't forget that somebody was her accomplice. And he may have killed Boyd's boy Charlie."

Lizzie sat down her coffee cup. "How can we find out who was in on it with Becky?"

"Why don't we just go ask her," said Aggie as she finished off her chocolate milk. "The Town

Hall is only a block and a half away."

≈ ≈ ≈

They stopped by the police station on the way and picked up Bootsie's husband. He strapped on his gunbelt, pulled his cap over his balding head, and joined the parade up the sidewalk to the Town Hall.

Jim Purdue was thinking that the state boys were sure going to be irked if he solved both the murder and the theft. Jim had to admit he'd like that. Neil Wannamaker was just too darn pushy for his liking. The Nail indeed!

They found the pretty blonde at her desk, stationed just outside Beau Madison's inner sanctum. She looked up as the entourage entered and muttered, "Uh-oh."

"Becky Marsch," said Chief Purdue, "why didn't you tell me that you're related to the woman who created that missing quilt?"

"Uh, I'm only distantly related. Not enough to count."

"You must have thought it counted for something," interjected Cookie Bentley. "You updated her genealogy chart only last week."

"That doesn't mean I stole the quilt."

"Makes you our Number One suspect,"

countered the police chief. "I think the SBI's gonna want to talk with you, young lady."

"Okay, I did it," she gave in. "But I don't have the blasted thing."

"Who does?"

"Bern Bjorn. He took it."

"Bern?" said Chief Purdue. "We had him in custody only yesterday." It irked him that Bjorn had been Lt. Wannamaker's chief suspect. The Nail would never let him live this one down, letting Bjorn go for lack of evidence.

"Why would Bjorn do a fool thing like stealing the quilt?" asked Beau Madison. The mayor had come out of his office when he saw all the people gathered around his secretary's desk. "Bern's the manager of the Dairy Queen, for gosh sakes."

"Just got a confession," said the police chief. "Becky and Bern Bjorn did it."

"Y-you're sure?" sputtered the mayor. Bern Bjorn was a leading citizen. He'd been in Beau's office the day before the robbery for a meeting of the Town Square Beautification Committee.

Becky Marsch started to cry. "Bern's my boyfriend. I did it for him."

"Aha, your mystery man," said the police chief. Her alibi had been that she'd spent the night with her boyfriend. But she'd never named the man. And small-town decorum had kept Jim from asking.

"I've been seeing Bern off-and-on since he and Wanda split up," she sniveled.

"So you talked him into stealing the quilt?" said Maddy.

"No, the other way round. Stealing the quilt was *his* idea."

"Bern's idea?"

"Yes," she nodded firmly. "His son Pinky translated the symbols on that ratty old quilt. Told his dad what it said, that there was a treasure buried in my great-great grandmother's well. He took the quilt so nobody else would be able to figure out the secret message."

"We have lots of photographs of the Wilkins Witch Quilt," offered Cookie. "That's how we figured out what the runes said."

"Guess he didn't think of that. Bern's no genius, that's for sure. A miracle he has such a smart son."

"Pinky's a clever boy," agreed Bootsie. "I had him in a few classes last year."

Becky nodded. "True. But he needs to get out more. Always playing those stupid video games.

Living off potato chips and Pepsi-Colas. The only friends he has are geeks just like him."

"Without those video games, he'd never have learned how to read runes," Cookie pointed out.

"Charlie Aitkens got it right," said Lizzie, whose husband had overheard the conversation while under the bridge. "A kid with a single mother figured out the message and told someone. But it turns out he told his dad, not his mom's boyfriend."

"It's only natural he'd confide in his dad," sniffled Becky. "Pinky doesn't particularly like Teddy Yost."

Chief Purdue pressed on with his questions. "You're saying you didn't want the quilt for yourself?"

"Why would I want that old rag?"

"Well, for one thing, it's worth a hundred thousand dollars. Some people might find that pretty tempting."

"Particularly a great-great granddaughter who thought the quilt rightfully belonged to her family," added Maddy.

"Poo," replied Becky. "That Viking treasure will be worth millions, so why worry about an old quilt?"

"There is no Viking Treasure," Maddy told her.

Becky Marsh turned to Cookie. "Mrs. Bentley, you're the town historian. Tell her she's wrong."

"Sorry, honey. There's no conclusive proof Norsemen ever made it to the Midwest."

"But my cousin Maury says —"

"So Maury Seiderman's in on this too?" said the police chief.

"Of course he is. I asked him to help Bern find the treasure. My cousin's a little nutty, but he's been chasing treasures all his life. He's fixated on witches and goblins and ghosts and buried treasures. He's a one-man paranoid organization."

"Don't you mean 'paranormal'?" corrected Maddy.

"No, I think she's got it right," said Chief Jim Purdue. "My night guy says Seiderman has been blathering about how Mad Matilda is gonna come save him from false imprisonment. False imprisonment ... in a pig's eye."

Aggie yelped, "What is it with pig's eyes?"

"Mad Matilda certainly seemed fond of using them in her potions," said Lizzie.

"I think I can answer that," grinned Cookie. "According to YourAncestors.com, Matilda Süderdithmarschen's family came from St. Paul,

Minnesota. They were chased out of town for being witches. So those potions we found were actually curses on the people of St. Paul. Before its current name was established, the city of Saint Paul was known as Pig's Eye."

"You're making that up," accused Lizzie.

"No, really. It was nicknamed after a one-eyed tavern keeper, Pierre 'Pig's Eye' Parrant. Today there's even a Pig's Eye Brewing Company in St. Paul."

Bootsie was confused. "Then why would she bury one those curses under the foundation of the Church of Avenging Angels?"

"Simple. The Avenging Angels were witch hunters, a threat to Mad Matilda. So she put a curse on them. Rev. Billingsley Royce was originally from St. Paul."

"How do you know this?" challenged Bootsie.

"From *A Personal History of Caruthers Corners and Surrounding Environs*. It says Rev. Royce came from St. Paul. Page 321."

"That's true," admitted Becky Marsch. "My ancestors came here from St. Paul. They were run out of Minnesota by those witch hunters who called themselves Avenging Angels. Those creeps even followed the Süderdithmarschens to Indiana."

"And they killed Mad Matilda?" asked Lizzie.

Becky nodded. "Matilda's mother and father died in the Great Tornado of 1889. And a few years later her husband was killed in a farming accident involving a mule. Kicked him in the head. So that left Matilda alone with her daughter to face those religious zealots. They killed my great-great grandmother for the Viking treasure she'd discovered in her well."

"I told you there's no Viking Treasure," Maddy said gently, patting the young woman's hand. "That was just a silly legend. We would have found it if there had been a hoard of hack silver around here. We've certainly looked."

"No, you're wrong. A family friend named Reggie Evers took Matilda's orphaned daughter Griselda – my great grandmother – and raised her as his own. Griselda recalled seeing the silver as a child. 'A dozen or more thin shiny bars that reflected the sun like a mirror,' she described them in her diary."

"Reginald Wentworth Evers was a Master Warlock who lived near Burpyville," remembered Cookie.

"Warlock, ha!" snorted Becky. "Reggie Evers

and the Süderdithmarschens were members of *Seiðr.* That's an Old Norse religion based on Germanic paganism. You can find references to it in *Eiríks saga rauða.*"

"In what?" said Beau.

"*The Saga of Erik the Red,* an account of Norse exploration of the Americas."

"You seem pretty up on all this stuff," observed Lizzie.

"Family tradition," Becky said modesty.

Chapter
Twenty-Seven

Crooks in the Can

After locking Becky Marsch in one of the police station's two holding cells, Deputy Pete Hitzer picked up Bern Bjorn and put him in the other one with Maury Seiderman. Lt. Neil Wannamaker was on his way down from Indy to pick them up.

"Gotcha, did they?" Seiderman greeted his cousin's boyfriend. He'd already claimed the top bunk, giving himself an on-high vantage point.

"Becky squealed on me," Bjorn spat out the words. He glanced angrily in her direction.

"No, honeybunch, I didn't," she called to him. "They had us dead to rights. They knew you killed Charlie Aitkens to shut him up about your stealing the quilt."

"Shut up, Becky! Don't say that in front of them."

"What? That you killed Charlie? You never

should've told your buddies about stealing the quilt in the first place."

"Charlie was gonna help me sell it. Said he knew a guy in Cincinnati who fenced stolen goods."

Becky threw a shoe at him. It bounced off the cell's bars. "I thought you were only interested in finding the Viking treasure."

"That's true," he replied. "But I'm not going to turn away a hundred grand. The quilt had served its purpose."

Maury Seiderman slid off the top bunk, landing on the floor like a 6' 3" tomcat. "Hold on, chum. You didn't tell me about the hundred grand. I want my share. You promised me a third of whatever we got."

Bern Bjorn backed away from the threatening figure. "Your share, I was taking about the treasure."

"Well, there *is* no treasure, according to these old biddies."

"Who are you calling biddies?" protested Bootsie Purdue, standing next to her husband.

"You and your quilting pals," shouted Seiderman. "You've bollixed up this whole deal. Now I'm mixed up in a murder."

"Keep talking," grinned Chief Purdue. "We've

got a station-full of witnesses." He gestured to the members of the Quilters Club. "No way you're walking away from this one. But it might go easier on you, if you tell us where to find the Wilkins Witch Quilt."

"I told you my great-great grandmother wasn't really a witch," shouted Becky. Angry about this turn of events. Being arrested. Her boyfriend turning against her. The treasure still out there unclaimed.

"Who cares whether the old hag was a witch or a Presbyterian," said Bern Bjorn. "I want to know where that silver is hidden."

"There is no silver," Seiderman repeated.

"There was," insisted Bjorn. "My son Pinky cracked the code of that message on the quilt."

"Your son has too much imagination," groused Seiderman. "Always playing those stupid video games. He probably made the whole thing up."

"No, Becky's great-grandmother saw the silver bars."

"That's true," she called from the next cell.

"Then where are they?" the skinny man challenged.

"I have a theory," said Cookie Bentley.

≈ ≈ ≈

All eyes turned to Cookie. She had everyone's attention. Even Lt. Wannamaker and the two burly state cops he'd brought with him.

"My theory is that a small band of Viking explorers made it here, having sailed across the Great Lakes from Newfoundland – or Vinland as they called it. They set up an encampment under the oak trees and dug a well so they'd have plentiful water. Or maybe it was simply meant to be a Money Pit like they'd dug on Oak Island in Nova Scotia."

"I've read about that," said the founder of the G.M.O.P.A. "It's been attributed to pirates, freemasons, and Norsemen. Some have speculated it holds a Viking treasure. Or even Marie Antoinette's jewels."

"Marie Antoinette wasn't a Viking," muttered Bjorn. He'd never liked Becky's know-it-all cousin. It had been her idea to bring him in on this treasure hunt.

Cookie continued doggedly. "Likely Mad Matilda's husband found the treasure while deepening the well. Word got out and Rev. Royce and his band of witch hunters saw it as their God-given right to confiscate the treasure from these spawns of Satan."

"*Seiðr* doesn't have anything to do with Satan," Becky objected. "Like I told you, it's based on Scandinavian mythology."

"Their religious beliefs must have got corrupted after a couple of generations in America," Lizzie pointed out. "The Wilkins Witch Quilts shows devils and angels doing battle."

"And she sold magic potions," added Bootsie.

The blonde had no response to that. So she sat down on her bunk to sulk.

"Old man Wilkins had been kicked in the head by a mule, so it was only Matilda and her daughter at the cottage. Stealing the silver was like taking candy from a baby. Rev. Royce and his followers dumped Matilda in the well and walked off with the loot."

"But legend has it they buried the silver under the doorstep of their church," said Maury Seiderman, his face pressed against the bars. "And you didn't find it when you dug around the foundation. I was there, remember?"

"That legend also said Rev. Royce planned to come back for it," remembered Maddy. "Perhaps he did."

"Exactly," chimed Cookie. "That Viking treasure is long gone."

"Damn," cursed Bern Bjorn. "All this for nothing."

"You've got the quilt," whined Seiderman. "I want my share of that."

"Nobody will be getting a share," snapped Lt. Wannamaker. "You can't profit from stolen goods."

Bjorn flashed a wicked grin. "Yeah, but I've got the quilt. You'll never see it again if you don't let us walk."

"Might cut some slack for little missy here and your weird friend from Chicago," said The Nail, "but no way you're going to walk on a murder charge."

"Wasn't murder," argued Bjorn. "It was an accident."

"Oh, that rock fell out of the sky and landed on Charlie Aitkens's head," scoffed Chief Purdue.

"No, Charlie was showing me this rock he'd found out in the field. Had some kind of writing on it. Like those markings on the witch's quilt. He was starting to figure out there might be more going on here than stealing a ratty old quilt."

"So you killed him," said Bootsie.

"Not just like that. He attacked me and I took

the rock away from him and hit him with it. Didn't mean to kill him."

"That's your defense?" said The Nail. "Good luck with that."

"It's the truth."

"Tell it to the judge."

Bern Bjorn set his jaw stubbornly. "Then you'll never see that quilt again."

"I think I know where to find it," said little Aggie who'd been taking all this in.

Everyone turned to stare at the eleven-year-old girl. In the excitement they had forgotten she was there. "You do?" said her grandmother.

"Maybe. Mr. Bjorn said Charlie was going to help him sell the quilt. They had their fight in the Aikens Produce barn. Why not look for it there?"

"We searched the barn at the time of the murder," said Deputy Hitzer.

"But were you looking for a quilt?" asked Aggie.

"Well, no. I was looking for clues to the murder." This was the young policeman's first wrongful death case. His enthusiasm exceeded his experience, as Chief Purdue would later say.

"We'll take another look," said Jim Purdue, "with an eye to finding a missing quilt."

Bern Bjorn cursed again. "Damn, I may as well tell you. It's hidden in a stack of horse blankets in the tack room. The Aitkenses don't keep horses no more, so it could've sat there till Kingdom Come if this pint-sized Quilters Clubber hadn't stuck her nose in."

Aggie smiled, showing her missing tooth. Happy to be recognized as breaking the case for the Quilters Club. "Thank you, Mr. Bjorn. I hope to see you next time I come to the Dairy Queen for a custard parfait."

"You might have to wait thirty years to life for that," said Lt. Neil Wannamaker, his dry wit going over the young girl's head.

"*Hmmpt*, I might not be there," said Bern Bjorn, "but you tell Maisie the counter girl I said to give you extra sprinkles. You're smarter than the lot of these lawmen. You're the one who deserves a reward."

"Gee, thanks, Mr. Bjorn."

"No reward has been posted –" began Lt. Wannamaker.

"Sprinkles will do," said Aggie.

Epilogue

It Turns Out Well

The Wilkins Witch Quilt was eventually restored to the wall of the Town Hall. It had been found exactly where Bern Bjorn said, folded in a stack of horse blankets.

Bjorn was found innocent of negligent homicide, the jury buying his story about hitting Charlie Aitkens during a struggle over the rock. Nobody in Caruthers Corners believed that yarn, but juries in Indy don't get very indignant about small-town fisticuffs that end with tragic results.

Nonetheless, Bjorn and his girlfriend Becky Marsch left the area. Some said they went to live with her cousin Maury in Chicago. Becky and her cousin had received suspended sentences as accessories after the fact.

Rumor had it that Boyd Aitkens had hired a hitman to avenge his son's death, but that was never proven. Nor was there any reports of Bjorn's demise.

Aggie did get the extra sprinkles until the

Dairy Queen closed down. Bjorn's ex-wife took over the franchise, but she let her boyfriend Ted Yost run it. He was not a very good businessman, as it turned out.

Maddy's son Bill and his wife made a full recovery. Kathy still walks with a slight limp. N'yen was excited to see them when they drove down from Chicago to take him home.

"It was a great visit," he exclaimed. "I got to join the Quilters Club and we solved a big murder case."

Kathy patted him on the head, convinced his imagination had gone wild. "That's nice, dearie," she said as he climbed into the car, a new Subaru courtesy of the trucker's insurance company.

Bill eyed his mother, suspecting there was more truth to the story than not. During their recovery they had not watched the news on TV, so they'd missed the frenzied coverage of the murder trial. The TV networks had had a field day with the witching angle. Nancy Grace did a segment from the Indianapolis courthouse steps. Piers Morgan had interviewed Christine O'Donnell about witchcraft, with her walking off his show for a second time. Anderson Cooper got an exclusive with Becky Marsch, talking about her great-great grandmother Mad Matilda Wilkins.

The story about the Viking silver never came out. The prosecutor had thought it too diverting a topic to introduce into the trial. Professor Ezra Pudhomme was disappointed, for he'd hoped to be interviewed about runology and how he'd helped crack the case.

Cookie Bentley did some more research on Rev. Billingsley Royce, leader of the Avenging Angels. He seemed to have disappeared from history after the 1899 murder of Matilda Wilkins. However, she did find a reference to the formation of a brewery in St. Paul at the turn of the century called Royce's Beverages. Its motto was "Beer Fit for the Angels." She wondered if it had been financed with Viking hack silver.

Royce's Beverages went bust in the 1920s, and records were lost in a fire. Particulars about its ownership were sketchy.

Freddie's daughter Donna was cast as Snow White in a kindergarten play. The Haney Bros. Zoo where Freddie worked part-time as a clown got a new elephant, this one named Rosie. She made a good mate for Happy, the circus's original pachyderm. An aging lion named Growly was also added to the menagerie. Bombay Martinez was happy with his new charges.

Tilly announced she was pregnant again. Mark the Shark was already handing out cigars. Aggie rolled her eyes at the thought of another sibling.

Boyd Aitkens was good as his word, offering to put up the campaign money for Beauregard Hollingsworth Madison IV's next mayoral campaign, but Beau surprised everybody by deciding not to run. Mark Tidemore announced his candidacy, and with Beau's endorsement was a shoo-in.

Lt. Neil Wannamaker nominated Aggie for an Honorary Lawman of the Year award. She was all giggly at the idea. She viewed it as validation of the Quilters Club as *real* detectives.

The Nail also had offered to nominate the other Quilters Club members, but they didn't have time for such nonsense. Maddy, Cookie, Bootsie, and Lizzie were much too busy, already planning the quilting exhibit for the next Watermelon Day festival.

↗ ↗ ↗

Thank you for reading.
Please review this book. Reviews help others find me and inspires me to keep writing!

If you would like to be put on our email list to receive updates on new releases, contests, and promotions, please go to AbsolutelyAmazingEbooks.com and sign up.

About the Author

Marjory Sorrell Rockwell says needlecraft arts – quilting, crocheting, knitting – are pastimes every woman can appreciate. And she particularly loves quiltmaking. "It's like painting with cloth," she says. But when not quilting she writes mysteries about a midwestern sleuth not unlike herself, a middle-aged lady with an unpredictable family and loyal friends. And she's a big fan of watermelon pie.

Bonus

By going to the Absolutely Amazing eBooks online website (AbsolutelyAmazingEbooks.com) and entering the password below into the Bonus Reward Section, you can access recipes for many of the dishes you read about in this book – for free!

AA1052

ABSOLUTELY AMAZING eBOOKS

AbsolutelyAmazingeBooks.com
or AA-eBooks.com

Made in the USA
San Bernardino, CA
18 December 2013